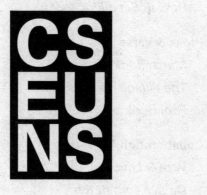

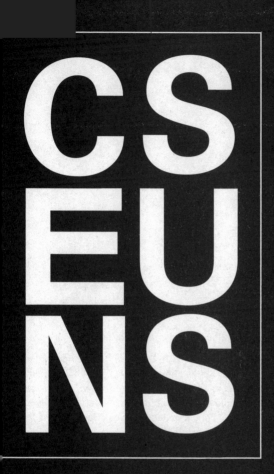

CENSUS

JESSE BALL

An Imprint of HarperCollins *Publishers*

CENSUS. Copyright © 2018 by Jesse Ball. All rights reserved. Printed in the United States of America. No part of this book may be used or reproduced in any manner whatsoever without written permission except in the case of brief quotations embodied in critical articles and reviews. For information, address HarperCollins Publishers, 195 Broadway, New York, NY 10007.

HarperCollins books may be purchased for educational, business, or sales promotional use. For information, please email the Special Markets Department at SPsales@harpercollins.com.

A hardcover edition of this book was first published in 2018 by Ecco, an imprint of HarperCollins Publishers.

FIRST ECCO PAPERBACK EDITION PUBLISHED 2019.

Designed by Renata De Oliveira

Library of Congress Cataloging-in-Publication Data
has been applied for.

ISBN 978-0-06-267614-6

19 20 21 22 23   10 9 8 7 6 5 4 3 2 1

For Abram Ball

My brother Abram Ball died in 1998. He was twenty-four years old and had Down syndrome. At the time of his death he had been on a ventilator for years, been quadriplegic for years, had had dozens of operations. His misfortune was complicated, yet his magnificent and beautiful nature never flagged. He was older than me, though smaller, and I spent many years at his bedside in the hospital.

But before that time, when we were both children together, when he could still walk and play, although I was young, I knew that I would one day have to take care of him, that one day I would be his caretaker, and that we would live together, could live together happily. As a child I assumed that duty in my mind and it became a part of me. I forecast the ways in which it might happen. I even worried (as a boy) about finding a partner willing to live with my brother and me.

It occurred to me last month that I would like to write a book about my brother. I felt, and feel, that people with Down syndrome are not really understood. What is in my heart when I consider him and his life is something so tremendous, so full of light, that I thought I must write a book that helps people to see what it is like to know and love a Down syndrome boy or girl. It is not like what you would expect, and it is not like it is ordinarily portrayed and explained. It is something else, different than that.

But it is not so easy to write a book about someone you know, much less someone long dead, when the memories you have of him are like some often trampled garden. I didn't see exactly how it could be done, until I realized I would make a book that was hollow. I would place him in the middle of it, and write around him for the most part. He would be there in his effect.

The relationship that I imagined as a child, that which I would have with my brother when he was grown, was very similar to that of a father and son, so I decided I would write a book about a father, on the point of death, who travels somewhere with his adult son, and that somehow, in the administration of those details, in and between the words, I could effect a portrait of Abram, as the son, and in doing so, would allow others to see what such a boy is like, or can be like.

In doing so, I was able, in some sense, to reenter the thoughts and ideas I had as a child—those I mentioned a moment ago, about how I would end up his caretaker, and what that would be like. A life is long, and we are many people, variously, in our guises, in our situations, but some part of us is the same, and what I felt as a boy I find myself able to feel now—a sad and powerful longing for a future that did not ever come, with all its attendant worries and fears.

I imagine some of you will recognize your own experience in these pages. I hope that others will find it a spur to new experience.

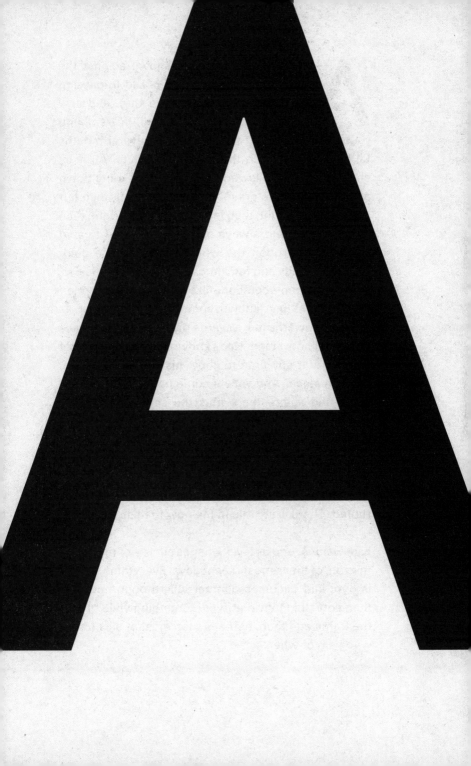

As I turned to lean my shovel against the rusted gray of the car, I looked in passing down into the grave I had dug, and saw there, along the face or wall, in trembling roots, the path I had traveled these several months taking the census in the farthest districts. As if by chance, my eye followed the slender red roots down and down into the grave, first left then left, then left then left, then right, then left then left, then right, then left then left, and always down. It was as if I could feel my hand upon the wheel, driving those field-wrapping roads and felt almost removed into the person I had been—someone like to myself, someone I myself might have known, someone bound in fact, as an arrow towards me, towards my heart and the place in which I now stand. Had I known him? Who is it that can claim at any time to know his own appearance, his own ideas? And yet we come back into ourselves again and again—there must be some recognition, something, even so slight. Must there be?

For me, I return to myself, I return and what I find is—that which surrounds me. The march of the hills that meets my eyes—it continues on within, uninterrupted. There is so little in me now to raise a cry.

I am waiting, and as I wait images circle—of my life, of my son, of these most recent days. Everything further is dim, and becomes dimmer still, though now and then something vivid arrives, something vivid breaks the frame and then, perhaps then most of all, I forget who I am or when.

Who can comprehend blankness? We as humans are so full of longing; what is blank eludes us. To be blank, to contain at your core, a blankness, it must be a talent—a person must have it, and must have it, possibly, from the very first. I have always had it.

In my time, I had read things, things like,

A census taker must above all attempt, even long for, blankness.

The fact that we mar our impressions, mar the scenes we enter by even our presence alone—it is something census takers carefully, gently even, pretend not to know. If we knew it, we could not even begin our basic enterprise. For us, the census is a sort of crusade into the unknown. Someone once said about it, *into a tempest with a lantern.* Into a tempest with a lantern—these are words I have said under my breath many times, though for me the feeling is not heroic but comedic. There is a helplessness to the census taker. The limits of what can be done are very clear. Perhaps it is this very element that draws those who do it to this terrible and completely thankless work. For it is clear that whatever good it might appear to do, there can really be no meaning in such a thing, much less in some infinitely small part of such an impossibly large endeavor. My wife, now dead, would laugh to see me in an old coat approaching houses. But, I feel it still, the warmth of the little lantern, the storm of the tempest.

Most of all it was my son who prepared me for this work, my son who showed me, not in speech, but in his daily way, that we are by our nature a kind of measure, that we are measuring each other at every moment. This was the census he began at birth, that he continues even now. It was his census that led into ours, into our taking of the census, our travel north.

It was his life, his way of thinking that made the work of the census seem possible, even inevitable.

But before that, before I went to the office to become a census taker, it happened that there was a notice given to me, not about the census, not about anything, but the opposite: about everything, a notice about everything. In some sense, a messenger arrived with an envelope and put it into my hand and at that moment I knew I was soon to die. In another sense, the way it would look from the outside, I was simply going about my business, I was speaking to a nurse in my practice, standing, gesturing in the hall. Next I knew, I was lying on my back in an examination room, and concerned faces hovered above, seeing me as if for the first time.

From there I went to see a physician, a friend of mine, who had a look at me. He poked around, prodded, stood scowling.

I could do tests, he said, but I think we both know what the tests would show.

He laughed. That was his way.

We sat there for a while, and finally, he patted me on the shoulder.

But your son, what will he do? Would anyone want to take him? Who would that be? Would he go to a group home?

The way he said the word *group home* was awful. I shook my head.

I said there was a woman I knew who'd made an agreement with my wife and I. Her promise was, she'd watch my grown son, take care of him if anything happened to myself, my wife. She lived down the road a short ways, was undistinguished, unimpressive, gentle, wonderful.

I was leaving the room, he was showing me out, and he stopped. He adjusted my collar with his hand and nodded to himself.

I think you should stop working. I think you should go somewhere dry, somewhere to the north, near Z. The trip would do you good. Think about it. There's no need to die where you lived. It's not nobler.

I got my son from the house he was at, the people he was with. They knew nothing of what had happened. I told them we were going on a trip, that my son would not be back for a while. They made a show over him about the trip, how nice it was to go on a trip. He was glad of it, and pleased. He had been building something with sticks, and he showed it to me. I told him I liked it, what was it. He didn't like that I didn't know what it was. Our house, he told me. Of course, I said, of course it is, I was looking at it wrong.

Back at our house, I walked around the rooms, from room to room. I thought, now I won't live here. Not even my son will live here. Somehow no one can live here now.

I left my son by himself for an hour and went down the road.

You do look like you'll die, she said. I never thought you would outlive your wife.

I've done it, I said.

But only just.

I'm going to take a trip, I told her. I'm going to go north doing the census. It will give us something to do, a last season together, a purpose that has essentially as much purpose as a thing can have, yet keep no purpose at all. My son and I can be together. We can see the same things and look at them. I'll keep close to the train line, and then, if things get bad, my son will travel back. I'll send word so you know to get him at the train.

She said it wasn't the plan she would have made, but she could see it, why I wanted it that way.

One last trip together, my son and I. And maybe I'll get better.

You might, she said.

I started to say some things about taking care of my son, about certain facts, or certain needs he had.

I know all this.

Just let me say it.

You can say it if you want, but I know it already. I'll take care of him, don't worry. It will be the same as it has been, whatever that was.

I know you didn't like my wife, I started to say.

It's your son who'll live with me, not your wife, thank god. Don't worry.

The next morning I went to the census office. I was there for a long time, and I left confirmed in a new appointment, a new profession.

My wife and I had always wanted to take to the road. Why don't we *take to the road* she would say. But somehow it did not happen. Although in a sense my son was the best possible reason to take to the road, he also prevented this taking to the road. At any rate, while my wife lived we did not and could not take to the road. Yet immediately upon her death I felt that there was nothing for it but to take to the road. It seemed I should find some way to do that, and the census was one way, a clear path leading nowhere and then nowhere and then nowhere and then nowhere. It seemed obvious suddenly: I could become a census taker, and my son and I could take to the road and there were no obstacles.

I got my son, and we went to the house, we left the house, we set out on the road.

I felt weak. I have felt this way for years, though. I have kept on, have worked when perhaps I no longer should have practiced, because I wanted to keep my son in a good house, with good things. Ever since he was born, our lives, my wife's, mine, bent around him like a shield.

For his part, he simply lived without regret. It is hard to feel someone owes you anything when they live without regret. What you do for them you do for yourself, isn't it so?

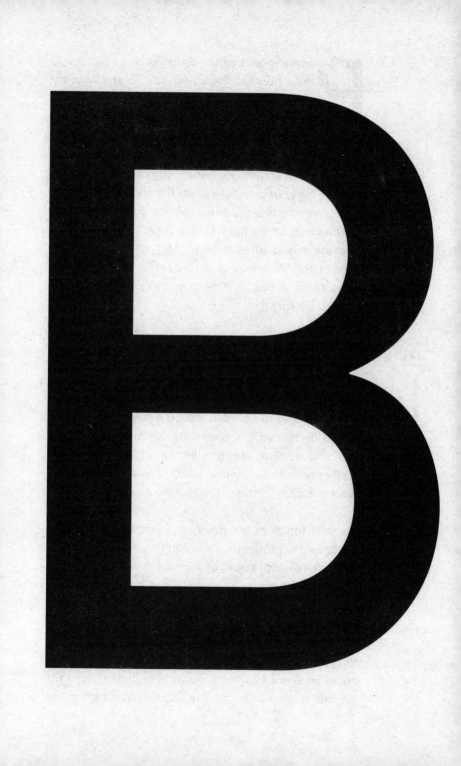

People would often come to greet us, out of their houses. That first day, in the country near B, we passed the outside of the circle— that which it could be guessed had been done, that which must already have been performed—a circle I observed in the offices on an enormous map a hundred feet across, we had gone beyond it—and so it was time to begin. I turned off the road and rumbled over a narrow drive to a high house, a house perched over its long single field. On the other side was a lake, and beyond, a forest's edge. Our car brought with it considerable noise, and this could be thought an advantage—for at no time in our travels did we take anyone by surprise.

They came, as I said, out of the house, a man and woman together. People come rather quickly towards you, don't they? And then they stop at a distance they consider safe—but it is never the same distance. I showed them my proofs, and the man laughed. He pulled up his shirt to show me the mark. *This here, the ninth census, and this here the eighth, this here the seventh. In the sixth and fifth I was prospecting— nowhere near it, and in the fourth I wasn't born.*

His wife too bore the mark, and I thanked them; we made as if to go, but they wouldn't have it. We must sit to some tea with them, and it was then that I learned a bit more about what it was, if not the census itself, then the business of the census. It contained things like this: sitting by the window of a farmhouse, holding a mug and looking out a plate glass window at a long lake where birds must throng, though then none could be seen. A sliver of moon was distant from us. A cloud made its way by. My son was occupied in the next room with some things they had found for him, he was singing, but when I finished my tea, we made our goodbyes and settled once more in the car.

How many visits should one perform in a day? How many miles travel? There are no definite answers in a work like this. We go where we can, do what we can, and ensure that our strength is kept up. That night we found a motel—completely vacant in the off season. *I can't make you pay,* said the owner. *Not when you're on official business.*

He was the first one I tattooed, setting the mark there on the correct rib. It is how we know if someone has been counted. There are those who say the census is barbaric, and they bring this as evidence. But did I not let a census taker make these marks on myself, and on my son, and on my wife in censuses past?

Each census has its own shape, and should sit upon an agreed rib. I suppose there is redundancy there, but not all census takers are doctors, so perhaps there was some worry that the wrong rib might be chosen. I feel it is well within the power of any census taker to find a third rib, or a fourth rib, but at the same time it has been my experience in speaking with census takers—myself as a private citizen—that they are often careless know-nothings. My wife used to say, they do this because they have nothing to do, no pursuit of their own. I felt the weight of this joke upon me when I took the job, for it signaled to me a kind of death. Would I carry the census always outward? At what point would I stop?

»

Gerhard Mutter, seemingly a man, but in fact, the pen name of Lotta Werter, who led a public life as the mayor of a German town near Stuttgart, wrote compulsively her entire life about cormorants. To her, everything applied to them. Whatever principles she discovered day by day, they seemed mysteriously entwined with those dark nimble eyes, with that whispering, wild ungraspable diving. It must be a terrible thing, she writes, again and again, in the same words (she uses the same sentences again and again—to the point where it ceases to be self-plagiarism and must be seen as refrain), it must be a terrible thing, she writes, to be a fish, and know that a cormorant has observed you. It isn't terrible to die, she thinks. It is simply terrible to be observed, and therefore to be somehow in helpless peril. There is no distance a fish can go, she writes, that will save it. From the moment at which it is noticed, the fish is permitted a sort of grace that will be concluded, excruciatingly, with the bayonet of the beak.

As I approached a house on the main road six miles past B, I felt that the census is in some way an observation, and if so, if it is, then what is its beak, when does the beak come, and what is the quality, if the beak could be taken into account, of the grace granted? Lotta Werter was also known for wearing a dark fur hat that she, by all accounts, would never take off. One or more of her biographers notes the joke that she would often make about the hat: *it is my wig* or *it is a wig* or *it is a sort of wig I wear.* She would often say this about her dark fur hat, which, in actuality was a series of dark fur hats that she purchased at a shop in Stuttgart itself. Seal fur, always, apparently. This fact is brought home by a page in Gold Ponds where she writes, *the seal is an obvious analog to the cormorant, but where the cormorant is patient, the seal busies itself with finding its pleasure, and so, over the course of a thousand years, becomes profligate.* What then does it mean that she wore a seal fur hat? A revisionary biography published in recent years brings this claim into doubt. Apparently there were no seal fur hats in Germany at that time. Such hats were invariably made from mink. There is a painting, however, which I have often looked upon, at the State Gallery in Stuttgart, of a cormorant perched in a tree, frozen in its indelible shape. The act of the cormorant's violence is woven into its trees and into the water itself—you could say, even woven into the fish that swim beneath.

The woman who came to the door was about thirty-five, and wore a loose sleeveless dress. She welcomed my son and me in, and we sat like three conspirators in her parlor, heads together.

How is it that three people can just learn to laugh, suddenly, at anything that is said? We were like that—drawn implacably to an unaccountable joy—and then spinning along its edges gratefully. She answered my questions. She had not seen the census yet—I was its first messenger, and so before I left I made our mark upon her. She opened her dress: the sort of thing that might confuse or worry an ordinary person, but for myself, having been a doctor, it was quite usual. I found the rib and made the mark. There was something she said—a story she told, it was, her house had been robbed once, she said, by a man she knew. She was in the house at the time and had stood behind the drapes. As they went from to room, the burglars, taking things, they spoke to each other, about the house and about her. She didn't mind at all, she said, the things they took. She had an inheritance of some sort—and didn't need much of anything. Or, anything she needed, she could buy again, and she might even like the trouble it took. But, it was this: listening to them talk, hearing them as they saw her belongings and spoke of them—it was delightful to her. She could almost have burst out laughing, so she said.

When the man described her to the others, and she could imagine their minds matching her to the house and possessions, a sensation of giggling—of permanent and proper situation in that which is oblique—came over her. To this day it has never left me, she said. She kissed my son on the cheek and embraced me fiercely when we went away. A terrible thing, I believe, had happened at some point to her right arm, but she did not mention it, nor did we. In the photographs by the door she—as she put it, *and here I am a bride, and here I am a bride, and here a child, and here a widow. But you are a widower—I'm sure you can recognize me in this photograph, however dark my costume.*

This is an example of the perfect accord of mind we fell into, the three of us. I had only to step through the door, only to introduce myself and showed my bonafides, and then, such a thing as that. I didn't realize until after—as we drove, and I mulled the encounter in my mind—but while we sat there huddled over the parlor table, she reached out and grasped my hand and I did not shudder, and my son, he grasped her withered arm. There is nothing that cannot be natural.

They call areas of Switzerland cantons. To my ear that has always sounded delightful. What fine things, I felt, as a boy, must be happening in the cantons. There is a constitution that some have, and I had it—to which everything foreign is wondrous, and all that is domestic, tiresome. I have often tried, in my reading, to look through the eyes of those who find in the most familiar things an endless reverie. I know it can be done. I have seen it done so often! But the turn—somewhere in it, there is a turn, and it is a turn I cannot make if I am not helped.

My wife used to say, all flesh is continuous. By that she meant—anything fleshed can mirror another fleshed thing, can feel somehow immediately anything felt, and that it is even sometimes possible to compel another to feel that which you feel.

The toll operator at the bridge between B and C, he knew her, my wife. I could scarcely believe it. He had seen her perform. It happened this way. We stopped the car and approached the tollbooth on foot, which in hindsight, was an odd thing to do, and I'm sure put the tollbooth operator on his guard. Nevertheless, we began our conversation in amity and it continued well. I explained what it was we were about. As a toll operator he seemed to feel that we were, as he put it, in the trade, and he was only too happy to go along with it all, although several times he had to stop to take tolls. Will you speak to them too? he asked, referring to the passersby. We will find them at their houses perhaps, I said. But what if they live far off? Wherever it is they go to, we will find them there in time. There is no hurry.

I showed him my proofs and he saw in the papers my wife's name, which is, it is true, an odd one. He said it out loud, my wife's name. She was my wife, I told him.

Yes, but was it her? Is she . . .

Yes, she is the one you are thinking of.

He related to us, to my son and me—how he had seen her in a grand theater at Weinau. That was before I knew her, I said. She had given up such things by the time we met. The man barked a loud laugh in spite of himself, recalling the grand theater at Weinau, recalling my wife's show.

I was very quiet, waiting to see if he would say more, but he said nothing, just stared and smiled and smiled again. He smiled again. He closed his eyes. He opened them. He smiled again. My son and I waited, leaned against the cheap wood of the toll shack. There was a pile of shit on the ground—probably from a dog. My son was looking at it—for there were flies congregating there, as many as angels on the head of a pin.

The toll operator was working his mouth, getting ready to explain what he was thinking. He had that habit some have—of preparing the listener with the seeming difficulty of his saying anything.

But, what was it like? I asked finally.

I had heard, he told me, about her clowning. She was very popular at that time. First, no one had known anything about her—nothing at all, and then, suddenly, she was very popular. I was newly married, he explained—living over a shop that I worked in. We had very little money or time. We didn't even have the clothing to appear in public really. The toll operator's face hung over the proceedings of his speech. You have been young, haven't you? You know what it's like. But, still I knew—my fiancée and I, we had to go. And then, the show was free—it was always free, your wife demanded that, as it turned out. I knew that she was a clown, but in what way—it was never clear, not even now. Is it clear to you? I doubt it. The performance was bewildering. Her impressions of life were . . .

He shuffled back and forth.

I think I had actually forgotten about this, he said. It has been years since I thought about it—and now here it is. Here it is again, he said.

We waited.

Her impressions, they were more vivid than what I could muster with own arms, my own legs. It was almost horrifying. I mean—you wonder what is in a body. How is it animated? How does it move? She did a thing where she invited someone onto the stage, and then she would mimic that person entirely until it was unclear which of the two was moving first. The mimicry was so complete that the subject ended mesmerized, as by a more perfect mirror formed suddenly from air. Finally, the person would struggle to escape it—to somehow stop what was happening, but by then she would *have them down* and whatever they did, it didn't matter. What was it the papers used to call her: a telepath, no, a physiotelepath—telepathic not with mind but body.

He trailed off. We looked at the ground.

But it cannot be true, he said—really, she was your wife?

I said that it was true.

What was she like?

I said I wasn't going to talk about that.

He said we must be about the same age, that his son and my son were of an age too. He said it was funny that her son should turn out that way, that she was a clown, and her son was, well, like that.

I didn't say anything, just started to leave.

He changed the subject. Farther north than there, he told me, people will not be so trustworthy as I might suppose. I should be careful.

He asked if I had some picture of her with me, something to prove to him what I said. Not that I needed to prove it, but, he would think about it again and he would like to be certain. Did I mind? I took a photograph from my wallet. He looked at it disapprovingly.

She is older there, he said, much older. I don't think of her that way.

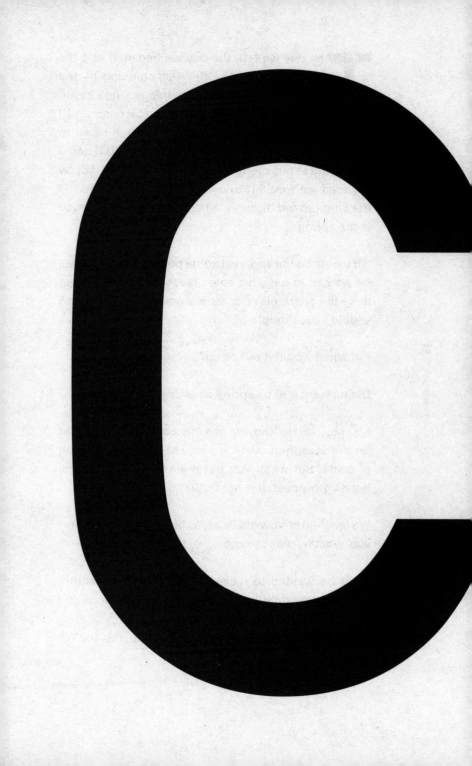

The day we left, the day we began, it was the first cold day. My son was standing by the door where the calendar hangs, and I stood there too. We looked at the calendar, and I turned it, and on each page, I said a letter. I said to him—and in this month we will pass through H and J and M and in this month through P and S and T. I drew the road we would take on a sheet of paper, and the drawing passed through fall and winter and emerged in the spring.

If it would be the spring at some point on the trip, then he wanted to have his spare glasses. I agreed about this—the spare glasses were a good idea, and one I should have thought of.

But when would it be spring?

Did he want it to be spring already? I asked.

No, no, no. He showed me his coat. He was eager for the season of coats. I, also, I said, like the season of coats. But when you get older you will find—the bones grow cold. It is not so warm as it once was.

We laughed at how old I was, as old as a grandfather—was what he was saying.

Then he wanted to leave the calendar on a spring month, some month we might return.

I reminded him—we were not going to return. We were leaving the house for good.

He began to cry.

We are leaving the house for good. Don't you remember?

In the next village, the third in a string of settlements that together comprise C, a woman sold us fresh bread from a little cart. Her advice was: eat your lunch by the canal; it's what I do. She said that the canal was built by a man named Holling, he and his lover, a man named Briggs designed it. They lived just up the road, quite a long time ago. Their studio is preserved. At the time there was the difficulty of them being two men, so she put it. But, they knew damned near everything that could be known about canals, and the plans they had made, that had been adopted, required their oversight for the completion of the canal (at that point already begun). So, everyone just had to swallow the confusion and let it be.

I remarked that any number of great men have been that way, and in fact, I joked, a number of them have even been women, whether in their own person, or in the person of their wife, who made them, did what they did for them, etcetera. She was not really listening to me, though, and did not understand. Will you repeat it? Repeat what you said? I said not everybody does what they are supposed to have done. Sometimes someone else did it for them.

Speaking is such a confusion.

We went to the studio. It was closed, but there was a large plaque with very small writing on it in brass. It appears that Holling was the more traditional of the two. He preferred golden sections, classical lines. Briggs was much younger and, as the plaque put it— found his inspiration in peculiar forms—animal intestines, photographs of bombed landscapes, worried children's toys. One of the main features of the canal was that it was not straight in any way. In fact, it served to string together disparate settlements, and wound around and through prominences of land. The idea was not to move ships from one watercourse or sea to another; it was for goods to move on barges. An odd side-prescription, put in also by Briggs was that fruit trees should be planted all along the track that runs from town to town the length of the canal. I thought of that part in Herodotus about a road in antiquity— where once a person could walk hundreds of miles in shade. That was in North Africa where shade must be a mercy.

My son liked this idea of the trees, and when I told him they had all been cut down he went off a short distance and didn't want to come back.

Well, I didn't cut them down.

There was a picture on the plaque, and it appeared to me to be an image, a proposed sculpture of Briggs and Holling embracing, seated on a bench. Whether the sculpture exists in truth or not, I can't say. At least we did not have time to look for it.

With a block of cheese and a persimmon (and our bread) we went down to the canal. As she said, it was lovely. We sat by a lock. The entire thing appeared functional and well cared for. I always get the impression of a grist mill from a canal lock, the five or six I have seen. It is the sense that you are partly inside of or on the edges of a large mechanism. It's like being in a clock—if that could be true.

My son touched the lock with his hands, and climbed on it. He wanted me to photograph him there, and I did. There is a pose he likes to make, sort of like a gunfighter, with hips jaunty and hands at the side. It is a very nineteenth century pose and comes from his love of those heroic days. He made the pose then. I have not developed the pictures, but I believe it to be an excellent picture. The light was falling just over my shoulder, and the texture of his sleeve was lit as if with a brush.

Ah—there was one thing about that lunch, and the persimmon. I will say it to elucidate his character.

When I turned away a moment, my son ate the entire persimmon. I didn't like that, I began to say something, I felt it wasn't the kindest thing he could have done—but then I realized, the persimmon should go to the one who will eat it in a gulp when you turn away. Persimmons aren't for people who soberly wait for their apportioned amount. That isn't the kind of food they are. A good lesson—we munched our bread and cheese in silence.

There were dead vines there by the wood of the lock and it was a cold day. Did I say that it was late in the year when we began the census? Perhaps that is a better beginning:

It was late in the year when we went with the census into the north country.

I think it is too dramatic however. I would rather go about the thing plainly—a plain description of how things have happened. In any case, it was cold, and we wore our coats generally.

When in the evening we came to a house ten miles on, how surprised we were to find the same woman there—she who had sold us the bread.

Yes it's me again, she said. You went the long way. The roads run in circles.

Is this where the bread is baked?

Yes, yes of course. Where else would it be baked?

She was not ready to let us all the way in, so we went about the full business in her entryway.

Are we done? Will you go?

Is there anyone else in the house?

No, no one.

I could have sworn I heard.

That was just me. I talk to myself.

What were you saying?

Oh, you know. Things you have probably said your-self.

»

My son likes for me to talk about my father and mother and to tell the stories of their lives. He never met them although he would like to—and asks if we can. They are dead, they aren't anywhere, I always say.

He doesn't pay attention to that part. For him they are somewhere, they are there when I tell the stories, and gone when I don't. It's fairly simple.

One story I tell is about a hat my father used to wear. My mother hated the hat. She wanted to get rid of it, but my father was always protecting it, hiding it, keeping it away from her, and then appearing with it on when they were about to go out.

It was a bowler hat, a fairly simple bowler hat, I don't know why my mother hated it.

In any case, she finally got her revenge. She found the hat one day when he was out. He hadn't been careful enough. She cut out the top with a pair of scissors.

My father's return salvo was to sometimes sit reading the paper in the yard with this absurdly compromised hat on his head. The hat has since been passed on to my son, who will wear it on occasion. When he does, we laugh together. We make the hand sign for cutting with scissors, and laugh and laugh.

Part of giving the census is being able to argue on its behalf. Not everyone will just agree. Not everybody will permit themselves to be marked. And this is especially true the farther you go, or so it seems.

As it happens, I found a good way of persuading people. I let them in on a picture of the census as an endless parade of census takers approaching them along the road. Each census taker will give an argument to them. Each census taker will want to thereafter set a mark on their side. Any one of the census takers can easily be put off. But how many are you prepared to argue with? For this reason, I say, it is best to simply get it over with now. Can't you see that?

If they don't believe me, I go into detail. I say, in the place where I was born, there are thousands like me. We sit in rows through childhood learning just one lesson—how to take the census in the most efficient way. We love no one, know no one. We are dispatched in waves, and travel, like waves, across the landscape, touching every last thing that may be touched, seeing every last thing that may be seen. The route that I have been assigned, it has been assigned to a hundred others, and that is just in this year alone. I am possibly the first of this census, but I will not be the last, I assure you. This census is to continue for a double-decade, twenty years, and in that time, you will see perhaps two thousand census takers coming down this road, stopping at your humble shack to bang upon its broken wood frame and call you to account for who you say you are. As the census goes on, the conditions become worse and worse. The census takers become colder, crueler. The environment in which they operate becomes more brutal. Everything—every last thing becomes worse. Perhaps it is better to have to deal with me—the kindest of them all, or perhaps not the kindest, but the kindest to you? No one else cares as much as I do. Then when the others come you may call to them as one who has been embraced, and they shall go on gladly. You will never be accosted, never.

I am not sure that it is a very good argument, but it turns out to be persuasive.

When I came up with the argument, I was a bit concerned about its veracity, as, in so far as I understand the matter, there are not and will be no other census takers assigned to this region. But, then I considered the matter metaphysically and then I considered the matter metaphorically and what I came to was: certainly though no one will come, there is a way in which each person wants to be known, and if this person permits some basic misanthropy (basic to us all) to rise up in himself or herself and thereby thwart the census, then it is only to himself, to herself that he or she does harm. How sad that would be. Then that person could only wait in the hopes that another census taker would come. So, I am merely stating the opposite of what is true, and as they say in hell, a thing can only be as true as its opposite.

If someone will on no account be questioned, if someone wants nothing to do with it at all, then I put a little tally on a map indicating the place where the refusal occurred. As I find it intensely pleasurable to mark down these refusals, I feel a great ambivalence about the work of the census, and am never put out or displeased, however it goes.

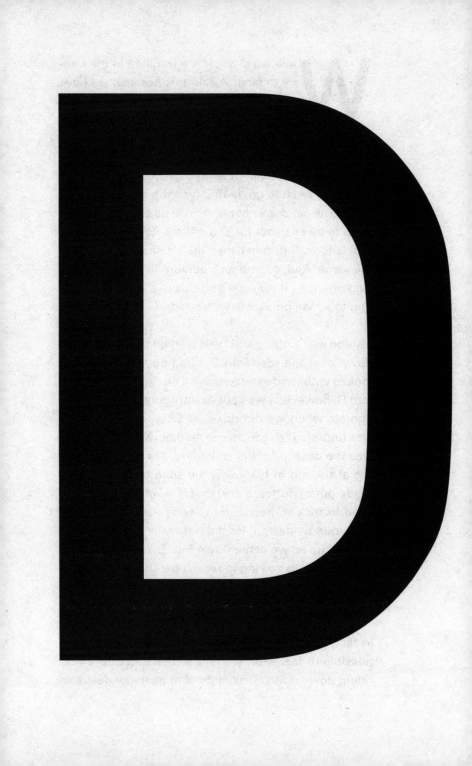

While we drive, it is a tradition in the family to sing. We do this because we have never had a car with a radio. I think it costs more to have a radio, or did once, and we got used to that. Since then—always, no radio. The car should be a kind of mechanical mule, I think. By that I mean—it should get you slowly to the place you need to go, faithfully to the place you need to go. The car does not need to go quickly. It does not need to be as beautiful as a mule is, for I like the way mules look. But, other than that, it should be largely the same. And, of course, a person riding a mule and singing—isn't it obvious that this is a superior situation to a man on a mule with a radio?

My son was singing and I was singing too as we came down over the road into D. I had both dreaded and looked with fond expectation on our imagined arrival into D, however, I was not exactly sure where D was, and so, when we did drive, as I say, down into it, I was unprepared. You see, my father was from D. This was the country of his childhood. My son was singing at the top of his voice, the song is about a cow made out of butter, a cow that is a kind of trick—it is used to trick someone in the song—and the song is very loud by design. He did not really care for being hushed up as we came down into D, but I really had no choice. I was trying to remember things my father had told me thirty years before—things I had most likely forgotten.

In fact, the town was unremarkable. In a sense, it is possible to feel what wild-horsemen must have felt, riding down upon cities in the dim past: the desire to simply burn these mediocre places and pile the skulls, it rises in the breast when one beholds a paltry place. There is a dream that the place you await does in fact lie in wait for you. This is the dream of being a traveler.

So when you see some false thing, some shabby town in place of the vale you long for, well, burn it, burn it! Pile the skulls!

In this case, my father had told me a great deal about this town; I had on my own account learned much about this town, but not to the purpose of learning or knowing about it specifically, rather so that I as a child could know about towns in general, that was my purpose while listening to my father speak. It was for this reason that I could not, trying to remember what my father had told me, remember anything: all my information about this town was embedded in some archetype of the generic. I would have to deconstruct my very notion of *town* in order to know what my father might have said. It is not an easy thing to do.

Alternately, I could simply hope that the town would remind me of itself—of the version of itself that had been told to me. Sadly, it did not.

Nonetheless, as it was a town, we were there for several days going about from house to house. I was told that two hundred and forty people lived there—so we were busy.

Although it is true that the town was unremarkable, there were still people living there. It is often true in this business of the census that one discovers one lacks the power to call out of the people one meets that which is indeed most peculiar to each. Of course, it is this very task that the census requires, and so my failure to obtain the quintessence of any individual interviewed is a very real failure and one that redounds to me again and again. I must, in speaking to a person, know what is special about that individual, and that data must pass through me back to the offices of the census in such a way that what is most particular, most special about the nation, and indeed of all nations, some aggregate of all the particulars of its human population, that this could be known and felt.

The first in whom there was a spark, we found him on the second day. The second and third on the fourth day. The house of the first was a narrow building by a square. There was a fountain there entirely covered in moss. We knocked on the door. He answered it: a man with a great black beard. I explained our business. He ushered us in to a wide room filled with tables. All of the tables were piled high with wooden puzzles, cutting tools, board blanks, pegs, polishing instruments, paints and brushes, coils of string, wire and gut.

I am a craftsman, he explained. You make wooden puzzles? Yes, I make them.

They were beautiful, and quite beyond me. I have always been the very worst one at solving puzzles. I think it is because I give up right at the start. Right at the very beginning, when you would think you should muster up your forcefulness and make a powerful start, it is just at that time that I give up. It is just at that moment that I am handing the puzzle to someone else, or even, more sadly, it is at that time that I begin to handle the puzzle in an ineffectual way, in such a way that it is obvious I am not even really trying any more to solve it, but only expressing a kind of interest in it on someone else's behalf. If it happens that, by accident, at that moment, at the moment at which, in handling the puzzle in a ginger mincing useless way, I end up making inroads towards a solution—let us say, the first portion of the puzzle falls open, as does in fact sometimes happen—then when a person who is watching me, a person who also wants to have something to do with a puzzle, when that person reaches out to touch the puzzle, seeing that we have moved closer to its solution, as such people always do at times like that, my reaction is, rather than to pull back, as would be the proper thing to do—in an attempt to prolong the puzzle-solving—I on the other hand, demonstrating my poverty of nature, give the puzzle over immediately, that is what I do, I give the puzzle over immediately, despite the puzzle perhaps being virtually solved at the time. This is even more ridiculous when you consider that the profession of my life has been surgery—and that I was accounted for a very long time one of the chief surgeons of the area in which I lived. Nearly any operation that could be done to a person, I have been called upon to do, and for the most part, I have had success. Yet, in this business of puzzles, my determination can make no progress.

None of this did I say to the puzzle-maker, who, while I ruminated, was staring intently at my son who was moving around the room touching the different puzzles.

Is it all right for me to speak to him? He won't mind? He can understand?

Oh, yes, I said.

I mean, he won't go into a fit or something.

No, nothing like that. You'll see.

The man went over and spoke to my son, using lots of hand gestures, lots of expression. They had a pretty good time of it, looking at the puzzles, and an even finer time in the next room in the workshop. In fact, the man found some things for my son to do, to help him with in the workshop, and so, as I went about in the town those days on the census, my son worked in the shop with the man, and in exchange for that work, took with him a kind of drill when he left. I don't know what the drill was for, nor did he. I think not knowing was what made it emblematic of the puzzle-maker's shop. Although, my son's understanding of that shop was doubtless very different than my own—for I was only there an hour or so.

In any case, I went up and down the streets, census taking, and eventually, came to a basement where two runaways were living. There was the question of whether runaways should be counted. Some would say not. I took a different view.

The boy was a fast talker. He said that his father was an auctioneer and that's why. He's an auctioneer and that's why, that's how he said it, explaining the speed of his tongue. The girl said whenever anything goes wrong, he can explain it. I said that was a very useful skill.

The girl resembled a swan. I squinted my eyes and looked again. Yes, she was very swan-like. I told her that I would call her Polly Vaughn. She did not know anything about that, and so I explained—Polly Vaughn was a girl who went out and was in the bushes with her apron wrapped around her somewhere in England perhaps and her lover thinks she is a swan and shoots her and is put on trial for her murder. What happened then? she asked. Well, he wants to run away, but he gets this advice from his uncle, don't you leave your own country till your trial be done, for they never will hang you for the killing of a swan. But she wasn't a swan, said the girl. That's right, I said. I have always disagreed with the opinion expressed in the song—although some say that what the uncle is actually saying is that whether she is a swan or a girl, it is essentially all the same, and either way he will be acquitted.

They knew nothing about the census, so I explained it all, we went over everything, and then I marked them. The girl was stoic, but the boy made a cry when the needle marked his side. I asked them about their plans. They explained that they were going to head in the opposite direction that I was going. They were of the opinion that if a place could be found that had as many people in it as possible, then such a place would be for them. They wanted my advice on getting to such a place. I said it is not just about getting there, but also about what to do once you are there. The boy was adamant that his fast talking would be enough. I felt looking at him that it might well be true.

I told them that my father had left this region some seventy-five years before, and that by following the very plan that they were bent upon he had made his fortune.

The girl wasn't really listening, and she suddenly decided to join the conversation. She asked how he was doing, my father. What does he do now? I was confused for a moment. Then I said that he was dead. That seemed to make her feel uncomfortable about their prospects. I explained that he lived a long life prior to dying.

Oh, she said, when did it happen.

About seventeen years ago.

They looked at each other—their eyes pouring something, I don't know what, pouring it back and forth from one to the other. We weren't born yet, the girl said. Seventeen years ago, the boy said, she hadn't been born. And I, I wasn't born yet either.

I told them it was important to figure out what things were worth doing—and then to just do those things, don't do any of the other ones. People will try to convince you, always they will try to convince you to do things you should on no account do. Negotiating these terrible pathways full of bad advice—it is the principal danger of youth. That and suicide.

She said, she knew about that. She had thought about it a lot. Two of her friends had died that way.

»

The boy spoke up. He said, for children these days, suicide is like falling in love.

The girl agreed. It is like falling in love. It is like painting a new door on the wall of your bedroom and stepping through it.

I mean—to imagine that all this time, the door has been right there and you haven't seen it.

She was toying with a torn playing card, an eight of spades. She looked up suddenly.

But, I like being alive. For myself, I keep choosing that.

She said she knew a lot about plants from her aunt who had a nursery and she could do something like that. She could have a nursery too, just like her aunt. Everything in the nursery is the way it should be. Anything that isn't is removed from the nursery, so it doesn't bother the ones growing there. Yes, she could do that. She could sell flowers and plants. The boy said something under his breath, and she hit him.

That's small time, he said. Small time.

She whispered something to him.

When I left and went outside it had gotten dark. I made my way up the basement steps in the cold. There was a smell of mud, cold mud in the air, and it was dead quiet. I looked back, and I could see them through the broken window of the basement, sitting side by side. She was talking and running her hands through her hair. The boy touched her face and I went away.

It has always been hard, going places with my son. Much as I love to go places, much as he does, much as my wife did, it is difficult to do so because of the way that people behave towards him. Even something as simple as getting ice cream at an ice cream stand might not be possible. We might arrive at such a place, get in line, and think that things were going well. But time and again, some conversation begins with other people in line, or some children are there, poorly supervised, and they begin to heckle him, or simply everyone stares, and perhaps asks some hideous question, some completely unnecessary question, and although perhaps it is still possible to get ice cream at this ice cream stand, it has ceased to be possible to do so pleasurably, and so we go back to the car, we get into the car, we drive to the house, and at the house we go inside and sit. Every time, my son goes happily to do something in another room, leaving my wife and I full of the sense of it—the way that our human specialty, alienation, expresses itself so gently, so generously, so thoroughly.

As we got older, we grew used to this. Perhaps we gained a thicker skin. Does that mean caring less? I think it does—but about everything.

These thoughts struck me as my son and I stood at the window of an ice cream shop in D. There we stood and I remembered specifically a painful incident that had happened twenty years before. It isn't worth mentioning, though, because it is like every other such incident. None of them have any character. It is so easy for humans to be cruel, and they leap to it. They love to do it. It is an exercise of all their laughable powers.

No one in D remembered my father. A common theme was, if the subject came up that my father had lived there a lifetime ago, they would mention someone, now dead, someone they had known, someone who probably would have known him. This is an excellent conversational maneuver, as it seems to establish a semantic bridgehead with which the conversation can go forward, when in fact the progress made is and would be entirely illusory.

At the beginning of the census, I had the same dream three times. Not since I was a child had this happened to me. In all three cases, the dream was just the same. It begins with an impression of having only then stood up. You have just stood up. You are in a living room. Behind you, there are people sitting, perhaps three or four. You know them so well that their details are not discernable. Someone is knocking at the door and you go to it. The knocking is louder and louder. You go through a set of rooms and down a hall. The knocking is so loud you can scarcely believe it. It sounds like someone is about to knock down the door. But, you feel no fear. You unlock the door. You open the door. Someone is standing there.

In the dream, it is my son who is standing there, but I am not myself. He doesn't know me. In fact, it appears to me that he, and I do not know him either in the dream, is looking for someone. But, there is no sound. I realized afterwards that there is no sound in the dream.

If there is no sound—then how could there have been knocking? I have wondered often about this—and I think it was a sensation of air, of the shuddering of air each time the knocker is struck.

You may wonder how it can be that we can travel so quickly when the business of the census ordinarily means that we must go quite literally *from house to house.* The truth is, we dispensed with that almost immediately. I will not say that I have abandoned my office as census taker. In fact, I feel, I take it more and more seriously. What I will say is this: in taking it more seriously, I know more clearly what it is that I am doing as a census taker, and this knowledge leads me to know that I do not any longer need to go to every house.

Unfortunately, when I explained what it was that we were going to do, I told my son that we would be going to each and every house. Now that our plans have changed, now that, in essence, upon seeing any house, we are faced with the option of either going to the house or not going to the house, my son has become immensely disapproving of the latter decision. Any and all proper formalities are welcomed and embraced by him. The idea that we would fail to do what we set out to do, he likes it not in the least.

So, we created a sort of pact, which was this—if there was a house that he dearly wanted to go to, we would go to it. However, I put in a caveat—he would need to say this before I stated my intention of going or not going. Otherwise, I am sure that he would simply have insisted upon going to every house.

»

Another problem came up when he wanted to return to a house that we had already been to. My feeling is that he liked the experience that we had in the house. An older couple lived there. They were very friendly. They gave us cider and something, perhaps maple sugar candy. In this case, I went along with it.

We went back to the house, approached it, knocked. The woman came to the door.

My son and I gave the impression of not realizing at all that we had been there before, and furthermore, of not remembering that now we were supposed to be acquainted with her. Although I do not believe that she understood this—she did not struggle. Her composure was perfect. She invited us in, and we reenacted the entire measure, cider and all. This time her husband was not present, but a woman, some cousin was, so I suppose it wasn't for nothing. I believe they thought it was some kind of joke, but decided for reasons of their own to play along.

This is a sort of proof of something I have long believed: that reason and sensical behavior are not always necessary if there exists some small flood of kindness.

The country was becoming rougher and rougher as we moved into the mountains. There was pine-forest, precipice, lake and stream, all drawn like lines in white ink. We bathed in a stream under a chalk sky, and it was the cold people sometimes speak of—that rare cold, the one you haven't felt before, that cold you can only feel once. People say they feel it when a ghost is in the room.

We stayed for three days at a lodge overlooking a waterfall. I had a Mutter book with me—*Geometries of the Dive*. It is a series of illustrations, hand-drawn, sometimes employing traced photographs. She took one tree, came to know its exact dimensions, and did the same with the cormorants that lived in the tree. She photographed them and drew them repeatedly. The book is to scale—on each page is the tree, and the pond. She desperately wanted to inhabit the world of the cormorant and she, Mutter, tried by any means necessary to approach it.

I imagine her, with her black fur hat, crouched on the opposite side of the pond, drawing instrument in hand, frozen in between tabulation, silhouette, longing. Although of course she was a prominent mayor and socially, therefore, extremely adept, although she had many children, three husbands, and indeed was acclaimed at the time as a playwright, I am still completely positive that her real desire was to leave her body and become in absolute terms a cormorant.

Most of us who want to become animals—what we want, in essence, is to be a human in any animal body. This is not at all what Mutter wanted, not at all. She, I am sure of it, wanted to be an animal that had never been a human. The cormorant that she would have liked to wake one day as, would never have known when it lay to rest the day before, that it had done so as a woman and the mayor of a town. Of course, even if it could be imagined that we could somehow effect a transformation into an animal form, the idea that we somehow would shed totally every last bit, immediately of our humanity—it is hard to feel what that would be.

Mutter writes of this when she writes, *the impression of dusk that a cormorant feels is nothing like our human dusk. We who are masters of nothing—who must change things in order to dominate them, cannot understand what it is like to be naturally, a master—to obtain a sovereignty that does not grasp, but extends in somehow palpable lines from the edges of every feather, from the point of the beak, the globes of the eyes. For us, we must diminish those beasts, those cows, those goats, that we would lead, we must break the brain of the horse that we would ride, so that we can crow that he lets us ride him. But anything changed becomes artifice, becomes less than it was, when it is made to suit the human hand. Our human victories by their nature have no glory.*

There is a set distance, my superior at the census office told me, that you will be able to travel. Do you know what it is determined by?

I did not answer.

Well, you could say on the one hand that it is determined by the total addition of all variables—your speed, the topography, human impediments, disease, etcetera. But, what I am speaking of is something else entirely.

Having been a doctor most of my life I had not had a superior in a long time, and it was very interesting to me to watch the way in which this man behaved, and to feel what it was to be something in relation to that. I felt that he knew things about census taking that I did not, precious things that I must know, and that I would in a very real way fail if I left the office that day without knowing them. I say this in order to explain the quality of attention with which I stood before him in his dim office. I may even have shifted back and forth, not out of uneasiness, but merely to display how much I was anticipating each new thing he would say.

He continued: the set distance that you can travel, whether you are young or old—you are old—is determined by the place of your death. You are traveling towards it even now. When I examined you and hired you for this work, not an hour ago, I did so not because I felt that you could become a census taker, but because I know that you already are, already were a census taker. You have always been a census taker. But now your efforts are joined to the community of work. He pointed to a wooden board. In serifed letters: *The Community of Work Goes Beyond the State it Serves.*

Do you know that the census bureau is older than the nation? he asked me. I said I did not know it. Do you know, do you believe that the census bureau will outlive you—will continue when you have gone? I said I hoped so.

He brought me to a huge cabinet full of leather-bound volumes, hundreds and hundreds. It went the length of the hallway. He knelt and began to take one out of its slipcase, but hesitated. It was too much for him even to come near the effort of so many lives.

This work. This work, he said. There were tears in his eyes. It is the real work, he told me.

I loved him then. But his hands were covered in the rings of different societies and I could not look at them. He raised his hands to make a point, and I shut my eyes.

I have always despised people who join societies. In general, I feel that groups of any kind are for the weak. The need for consensus is the most disgusting and pathetic aspect of our human world. Is there none who can simply wander alone beneath a sort of cloth tent painted with dreams?

The plan that we had, my wife and I, it was to live somewhere the three of us until, as she put it, the tree dies. Until the tree wears its leaves into winter. She spoiled the plan one morning when she took a nap. I was reading in a chair not three feet away. She must have been dead for at least an hour. I stood up, asked her what she wanted from the kitchen. She didn't say anything. I went to the kitchen, I came back—and that's when I saw.

The plan was that we would depart in the same breath, as on some joined raft.

This idea, which was such a great comfort, was proven entirely worthless when the life went on the one hand out of her and on the other it stayed in me. Perhaps that is why I chose to take this charge, the census, and travel, finally, with sure steps, towards something, even if I did not know what it was.

Telling my son what had happened to his mother was not at all what I thought it would be. I said it out several times, in several ways. Saying it to him I said it to myself for the first time. What he knows about it—about her being dead, isn't what I know, because what he knew about her being alive was different than what I knew.

He used to play a game where he would be a soldier. He would be out in the yard, roaming around in the bushes. There would be a battle and he would be shot to death, and he would slump there to the ground, against a tree, or next to a telephone pole. At that point he would be dead, he would have died in the military action, and he would know it—he would feel it, what it was, being there, taking part in that role. So, he wouldn't be in any hurry. Then, sometimes we'd get a knock on our door.

Do you know there is someone lying in your yard?

Oh, yes, we'd say—it's fine. He's just dead. He's playing dead.

When I looked at her body there in the chair, I thought: is she playing dead? Can she be tricking me?

The next place was surrounded with a high fence. It was a sad dwelling. I suppose you could call it that in fairness. There was a gate, and you couldn't get through it. There was no knocker, no bell. But when we stood there a while, someone came to the gate, and that's who let us through, a boy. Meanwhile someone else was watching from the house. I saw a face in the box of the window and felt—not in me—something hostile.

We got up to the house, we got into the house, to a room full of beds with a stove in the corner, and at that point we were asked to explain ourselves. So we explained ourselves, and in explaining ourselves, it became clear to the family, a family of six, that we were the enemy, or, if not the enemy, then the messengers of the enemy, the enemy that they had heard about for so long. This is my guess regarding what these people must have thought. It is my opinion that everyone who was not one of them was to them draped in poison. We appeared out of the south wearing green clothes of poison.

As I did my mistaken explaining, as I explained to them that we were there for the noble purpose of taking the census, I saw what was happening, but I had given my speech about the census so often, that it was not easy to simply stop.

There was a long silence punctuated by the sound of something metal slamming against something somewhere to the back of the house.

You're going to write down that we live here, and how many we are, are you?

I said that I was going to do that.

Through one of the windows, I could see the car away beyond the gate, which was still open. It sat there in the road, a few hundred feet away. I returned my attention to the room.

There were three children, two quite young, one possibly of school age. They approached my son and had the sort of encounter that children do. Even when there is no circling, there is a bit of circling in it, and often the matter concludes with all going off in the same direction. That's what happened. They all went off to another room.

We don't want to hear your questions, and we won't give you any answers. What's more—you don't put anything about us down, not for any purpose.

The other man, not the husband, leaned against the wall. He had a brutal face full of insult. He hadn't said anything yet. He had the hands we doctors recognize— hands made to hold weapons, hands never glad if they are not serving some deformed purpose. He was the one at the window. He spoke up,

maybe they don't leave without a real promise.

No one said anything to that, so he kept going.

You got your needle, old man? You going to put your needle in me? I'm not as stupid as you think. I've been to the south—I know what you do.

He came over and stuck his face an inch from mine: You're not putting your ink in me, not in me, old man.

I didn't move an inch, just watched him. People like this are small; it is almost always possible to escape them in those first moments, but once you consent then what is real for them becomes real for you and it is hard to find a way out.

He stalked back to the wall and slammed his hand against it, cursed softly to himself.

I thought very hard and thought of nothing.

I felt very clear at that moment in my stubbornness. The fact of it—of the implacability of my stubbornness, that I would not refuse it, my stubbornness—was obvious to me. Why it was that I was helpless in this case, well, I don't know why. Ordinarily I might have said anything and left. Maybe it was because I was just as happy passing on down the road and avoiding them entirely. But now that I was standing there, now that I had seen things, I couldn't unsee them. More than anything, I think it was because of the metal clanging against the house. I think such a simple thing as that—it rendered my brain completely useless. If you had asked me to play a game of chess I might not have been able to move the pieces. I would not know a knight from a rook.

I was standing under this low roof, almost partially crouched, looking at this man, and the others were waiting for me to respond. I think only a second or two had passed, we were living in the aftermath of his blow on the wall.

I said, you brought me in as a guest. So, what I see now, I won't speak of. But what I saw from the fence, what I saw before I was your guest—that is my own affair, and since it is my own affair I will speak of it to whom I like and where I like and when I like.

The wife's face turned white. The husband shook his head.

It was a kind of problem. The census was a kind of problem for them. We all looked at it and the metal clattering came again and again and again.

The wife said quietly:

Why do you take your son around with you? What's the purpose in it?

We stick together.

The woman started to say something about God cursing certain people, but the husband cut her off.

I was trying to figure out whether she meant that my son was cursed because of my job as a census taker, or on the other hand, whether, but the husband demanded my attention.

He had something to say, he wanted me to know. He proceeded to tell a story about how the sheriff had come up there once, that he tried to get something from them. The man asked me if I thought that the sheriff had gotten it. He asked the other man, too, did he think the sheriff got what he wanted.

The other man said that he got something. If it was what he wanted, who knew.

Seems to me, the woman started to say,

but the man cut her off again, his voice like a wet whip:

what does it mean to just come up to someone's house? Why do you think you can do that?

He shook his head each time he spoke. It was his preferred gesture.

I felt it was like when you are going down a hill and have begun to fall from a bicycle. It is hard to make plans about what to do.

Then there was laughter, just laughing from the next room, we all turned to look, and the children came back in, the older girl holding my son's hand happily. They stood there looking at us. There was a whirring sound and the clattering noise stopped. The children were so happy. Their faces reflected sunlight we couldn't see.

Their voices came, one then the other then the other.

How long are you staying for? How long are you staying for? How long? You must stay here forever, at least a week!

»

Down the road, actually around the very first bend, was a little cottage. A man of sixty lived there, with a face like a horn button. The three of us sat at his kitchen table and he offered us rum, which we drank. I told him what had happened at the compound.

He said, ten years ago, I was here when they came. It was just the two of them then, the brothers. Then came the woman. Do you know a funny thing? Anytime you see them—sometimes they go down to the town, sometimes they come around here to check up on me, like good Christians, anytime you see them, it seems like one of them, one brother or the other brother, like one of them is in charge, but it isn't so. That woman does whatever she wants, and she owns them body and soul. They are her mouthpieces, and whatever they say, they say it because she said it first. She grew up a dozen miles from here, and the list of things that woman has done . . .

He spat on the ground. It was his own house; he spat on the ground. He poured us some more rum.

It's for the road, he said. Rum for the road.

He laughed hoarsely, really not a laugh at all. Do you know this laugh?

The man brought out some pictures. This is a picture of my wife and daughter.

Aren't they beautiful?

Yes, very beautiful.

They were beautiful, they certainly were. Can't say they weren't.

Did they die?

No, they live somewhere else. You see, I can't be gotten along with. I am just a bastard some days.

And now the boy was trying to understand; he was being generous with me.

But you, what made you do it? Why would you stop being a doctor?

Some days had passed; we had traveled quite far, and seen several things, some notable, some already forgotten; now we were sitting on the porch of a large Victorian house. Beside it were many other houses, all old, beautiful, many built of wood and some of stone. We had emerged from the hills into a sort of basin, I suppose it was the beginning of E, and in the midst of the basin there was a rise of land and on it an old settlement.

There was a huge bank building across the way, and several churches. It had been a prosperous town for something like thirty years, so they said, a hundred and fifty years ago. Such brief blooms of wealth leave their impressions most in architecture—these outward signs of might. But like might, wealth is just a kind of pressure. Something hollow is left when it fails.

I sat on a rocking chair. My son sat on the steps. A small boy sat next to me in another rocking chair.

What made you do it? he said again. Don't you like helping people?

I did like it, but I wanted to do something else.

He understood that. He said that he thought about fossils a lot when he was eight, but now that he was nine, everything was different.

Somehow, he said, being nine, you can look back at being eight and see how clearly you had misunderstood things. He related to me how he would memorize fossils—their names and shapes, and write out the names in a book. He would get it for me if I wanted. He even owned one, a trilobite, as well as several plant fossils. He was not of the opinion that animal fossils are superior to plant fossils. His best friend, who still does fossils by the way, even though he is nine now, too, prefers animals. This is misguided because the animal fossils don't move. They aren't, the boy explained, about to move like a real animal. Did I know what a fossil was?

I said that I did.

Right, right.

His voice implied that he couldn't just believe me, not just like that.

His father came out and brought the papers he wanted to show me. They had moved to the town from somewhere else. This is the kind of thing the census likes to know. Actually, it is of very little interest to me, but when a person goes to another room to get papers, I just wait. I am learning about waiting for things to happen, really for almost anything to happen.

What do you think? the man asked. Is it enough?

Oh, yes, I said. This is very good.

»

As we drove that night, I told my son about the loneliness that sometimes afflicts people who are alone. Meanwhile, I explained, some other people are just as alone, but never become lonely. How can that be?

We thought about it for a while.

I told him that I was thinking about cormorants almost all the time because of my study of Mutter. All the books in the car were written by Mutter.

Bringing together the thought of cormorants, a thought that, even now, is still poised somehow in the air above me, with this notion of loneliness and its haphazard effect—it is almost as though some are drawn to loneliness, as to an art—we come to the woman of San Nicolas Island, a person who, it seems, did not so much suffer the horror of loneliness. Over the rumble of the car, I related the story of this woman with great delight, telling my son that she had been on the island for eighteen years when she was discovered in 1853. That, coming to shore with her rescuer, she wore a green dress of cormorant feathers, such a dress as had never before been seen. The dress, which had become her integument—like some sort of hermit crab shell, this cormorant dress had, seemingly improbably, formed around her, sewn together with binding of whale sinew—this feathered dress was the outward emblem of her plight, and in some ways constituted the main part of her available for judgment, as in other ways, she was somewhat ordinary—apart from her miraculous ability to survive.

He wanted to know where the dress was.

I told him the dress was in the Vatican, that because it was miraculous, because, in and of itself, it held the essence of what is unknowable, and what is therefore more valuable than value, what is invaluable, it was sent to the Vatican, a place known to be a repository for all that cannot be understood, but must be preserved. I said this was a kind of joke also because the dress is presumed lost somewhere in the Vatican. He did not laugh but looked at me steadily, waiting.

The road ahead of us was down and down and down. It was in a cleft, so that what we were going down towards—that could not be seen very well. Of course it was also the nighttime. I continued:

She had a song that she would sing to her rescuer and to others, *Toki Toki yahamimena / Toki Toki yahamimena / Toki Toki yahamimena/weleshkima nishuyahamimena / weleshkima nishuyahamimena / Toki Toki yahamimena . . .*

My son did not ask me what the song meant. The reason for this is: he doesn't ask that kind of question. The idea that someone could tell you the meaning of something that is before you—let us assume a thing is before you in its entirety and you do not know its meaning, and so you expect someone to give it to you—this is foreign to him. If there is something completely hidden, of which there is a small part—yes, he might ask. But, looking at a hare or a geode, he would not ask what it means. As well ask what a kaleidoscope means. What does it mean?

Nonetheless, I wanted to tell him about the meaning of the song, so I did. I said that there was much to know about it—and little. Someone translated the phrases as: *I live contented because I can see the day when I want to get out of this island.* But this is problematic for many reasons, most particularly that the translation was conceivably affected by knowledge of the woman's plight. It seems she had sung the song to an otter hunter, and that he in turn had sung it to a good friend of his, many a time, so that he too memorized it, held it in his heart, and it was that man who in turn decades later recited it for another man, with the marvelous name of Talawiyashwit, who brought us the above translation. A voice singing the words can be heard on a wax cylinder from 1913, which, incidentally, is the year on record with the largest number of deaths from lightning.

A different understanding of the whole matter can be had by adopting the view that whatever song she sang while on the island had two simultaneous meanings supported in the words. The first would be the ordinary content of the words, and the second, I live contented because one day I will leave this island.

Alternately, one could say that it is expressly because she was comfortable on the island that she did not die. In essence, she didn't need to leave the island.

Boxes have been found there, in the cave where she lived, more than a hundred years later, beautiful redwood boxes containing hundreds of artifacts, fishhooks, seashell dishes, ochre, soapstone ornaments. The house that she built out of whalebones was also found, still standing upon a rise over the sea.

It takes little effort to picture her some morning in 1841 watching such beasts as cormorants pass back and forth along, over, in the waves. She would have been about thirty, in the fullness of her life. If she did turn over those words in her mouth, *Toki Toki yaha-mimena,* and if they did mean something having to do with the day that she would leave, I wonder, as the years went by, if she began to conflate the time when she would leave the island with the time of her death, if in fact, the song could be, at the same time, a deep statement of life, and a plea for exit from that life. What could she have known of what would come if she did leave the island?

In fact, when she reached the mainland, she lived only seven weeks and was buried in an unmarked grave, and during that time she found it impossible to be understood by anyone, for there was no one left there who spoke her language. All she could do was to continue to sing and sing her song. I am curious how loud she sung it, whether under her breath, or with a ringing voice.

The human reaction to the epic is most manageable when it is elsewhere. Those mythic things that stand before us, shining, in dresses of cormorant—what do we have, what can we possibly offer in exchange?

»

Mutter knew of the woman of San Nicolas Island, I am sure of it. She mentions her somewhere, but for the life of me, I cannot find the instance. My memory of it is this: Mutter does her best to sever the link between the woman and the cormorants. She finds nothing germane in the dress of cormorant feathers. This utilitarian use of the bird's plumage might have been resourceful, but it demonstrates no comprehension of what it means to be a cormorant, so Mutter.

For her, the woman of San Nicolas Island is beside the point.

It could be said, however, that, if the woman dove in the dress, that the cormorant feathers, which resist water, could have been a fundamentally useful aspect of the garment. I imagine myself bringing up this point to Mutter defiantly, though I am quite sure that a conversation with another human being about cormorants was not something she would ever have tolerated.

The greatest disdain that Mutter could possibly heap, and she heaped a great deal, was saved for cormorant fishermen. The cormorant fisherman, extremely resourceful in a brutal way, loops a binding tie about the neck of a cormorant, one that he has taught to trust him. The tie is tight enough that a small fish may pass the cormorant's throat, but not a large fish. The fisherman then sits in a boat and waits while the cormorant dives and swims and does cormorant things. Eventually, the cormorant, in encountering all the various objects of cormorant life, encounters a fish that is a fine feast. He tries to swallow this fish, but finds that, strangely, he cannot. He is under the water, a fish in his mouth, and he is choking on the fish. So, he goes to get help for himself, and the person that he goes to is the fisherman. To the fisherman's eye, he sits in his boat and his pet cormorant leaps out of the water, fish in throat. The fisherman pulls the fish out of the throat, saving the cormorant. The cormorant goes back to what it was doing, leading it implacably towards another fish too large to swallow.

»

I do not keep much track of the days of the week, but I know that it was a Tuesday when we happened by accident upon a birthday party.

I know that mainly because the man's name whose birthday it was, his name was Tuesday. It was some prank his parents had played. He was named Tuesday, his brother Wednesday, his sister Thursday.

Tuesday came to the front door wearing some horrid birthday bib. He would have nothing else but that we join him and his family for the birthday dinner, which was a remarkably delicious meal. His own son, his daughter, his wife, his mother, all were present. There was much singing, but no presents. Tuesday apparently had everything he wanted. The present I ask for he said is that no one burdens me with presents.

We sat out on the lawn in chairs until it was well dark. My son was asleep. Tuesday offered we could stay there. I thanked him, but the feeling in me, overwhelmingly, was to push on. I wanted to get as far north as possible. Somehow this birthday of his made me feel that although I would not have another birthday of my own, I should push towards it, actually force myself through time towards the turning of the year. In this case that meant helping my son to the car, covering him in a blanket, and driving on in the night on a road that I could scarcely see. When the light from the occasional lamp illuminated the pavement it seemed too foreign to me, frighteningly abstract, both closer and farther than I could ever expect.

When you are a young surgeon, it often happens that you are put into situations that you did not imagine were possible. The set of things that could be wrong from the get go—before you are put into such situations, you would never assume that it could be true: that you would be in such a situation, and that you would be called upon to fix anything. You would think that it is totally obvious there is nothing to be done. And yet, by hook or by crook—or just plain chance, it comes to pass again and again that the very worst events come to pass, and it is on your watch. The nurses are looking at you. The other doctors are looking at you. Sometimes the patient, awake, is looking at you. Everyone is wondering—what will he do? How will he fix it?—never mind that sometimes no one even knows what "it" is to begin with.

The result of this is that one develops a sort of facility—I won't say one is prepared for the worst, because there is no such thing as actually *preparing for the worst.* However, one becomes used to the absurd idea that the worst things are being visited on you as by some supernormal agency, and that the best you can do is to try to weather the storm. Thus, if someone's leg has been crushed by a garbage truck, and you are looking down at this spectacle on the operating table, this spectacle of an operating room, this spectacle of you, scalpel in hand, considering what must be done (you are looking down on yourself as if from above) then it is not just a matter of feeling—how can this go right, what can I do to make this right, but there is also this other thing—that you think, life is truly absurd, and there really is no meaning, only objects of various size colliding in space, if they are so lucky as to be near each other.

The propensity for effective action coupled with abstract philosophical assessment was somehow strong in me—and only grew stronger with age, such that, in the years before I gave up my practice, the nurses and doctors with whom I worked had become very used to listening to peculiar monologues that I would give while operating. It became a sort of running joke—and was especially funny because the insight that I could obtain at such times was really much greater than at any other. If I were, for instance, at this moment to simply try to speak, I am sure what would come out would be nonsense, just pure drivel. However, at those times, while operating, I was inspired.

I remember the day that I was given my doctor's bag—a black leather bag with instruments in it. This was a very long time ago, I don't think anyone even possesses such a device any longer. But, for me at the time it was a very big deal, and I remember looking at it in horror, thinking of all the situations that I was now supposedly qualified to fix, having only this absolutely insignificant tool set. The miracle of medicine is that anyone ever recovers at all, from any injury, however small, and much of that is simply chance and the body's natural powers. In a way, we doctors are done a disservice by the faith that people put in us, for when things go well we are ignored, and when things go ill, we are blamed. But actually, we do not always have that much to do with it.

I remember the case of an old man who came in. He was complaining of pain in his arm. I examined him— this was in a small provincial hospital—and I noticed that his right shoulder was dislocated. I fixed it, and he was ushered out of the hospital. Two hours later he had returned, and why? Because his left arm was broken. The right shoulder, as he put it, had been that way for years. I had fixed the wrong thing.

»

When I signed the paper joining myself and my will to the mission of the census, I was told a curious fact. Those who travel on behalf of the census—not only do they have no special rights or protection, as do many other sorts of workers, but in fact, they sign away their basic rights of protection. Anyone may injure, attack, kill, harm a census taker and there is no legal recourse.

Why is it this way? Because the census takers must be seen to be completely harmless, even in so much as their presence itself might be harmful by dint of the responsibility one might bear for their presence. To wit—a census taker would never be admitted to a home if it were possible that he could sue for injuries sustained within.

This absolute lack of protection has at times led to the deaths of census takers in various places under circumstances which, had the census takers been ordinary citizens, would clearly be judged murder. What is the attitude of the census bureau to this appalling situation? If I had to put my finger on it, I would say, the basic idea that we are alive each one of us and acting to fulfill his/her own aims—it is an idea much disputed in the offices of the census. Rather they would say, the census is a large instrument made up of living cells—and each cell is a census taker. None of them is worth anything alone—but in total, well, you understand.

As for the difficulties that were immediately created, great difficulties you would imagine, of recruitment, it turns out that the mythos of the census taker was, if anything, enlarged, by the idea that census takers are utterly vulnerable. People are always looking for the new class of martyrs. In the census taker the modern martyr was found.

»

I kept some of the rules of the census on a little placard in the glove box. I don't know what the purpose of the placard was, or where it was intended to sit. In very neat print, the placard read:

If you are invited in to a house, you must go.

Never harm anyone with word or deed, even in defense of your own life.

Wear neat presentable garb.

No complaints. No sabotaging of the reputation of the census.

Never expect help from anyone. There is no help for you.

Once each month send completed documents to the center from which you came.

Something I had meant to mention, but forgot to:

The father of the fossil-hunting child, a man with pale red hair, told me in confidence that he had moved from another district far away because of testimony he had been forced to give, testimony in a criminal case. He had observed, in the street outside his house, a murder. He had not been alone in observing it. In fact, dozens of people had seen it happen. The trouble was, the murderer was a very influential man and no one would testify.

I had my wife and son to think of, he said. I didn't want to do it, but then I found myself agreeing. I found myself testifying.

Did you have to go to court?

I took the witness stand, and on the basis of my testimony he was convicted and then hanged.

But why did you change your mind—why did you testify when you had decided against it?

At this point his wife had come into the room. She was a small woman with pale eyes and lustrous, beautiful, almost obsidian skin. A rectangular hat sat atop her head and I was captivated. But she was watching him.

She watched to see what he would say to my question, and when he said nothing she laughed.

Why don't you tell him why you testified, why don't you tell the man?

She looked at me. It is a kind of riddle, don't you see?

She laughed and laughed. I like it so much, she said, the horror of our life—that brought us here. Let's say this, do you see that tree?

I looked where she was pointing, out the side window to a tall tree in a sloping park by the bank building.

I see it.

If the man were hanged in that tree this minute, and you could see him, you would know everything.

I thought about it a moment. Oh.

Yes, she said, still laughing. They were brothers, twin brothers.

She took his arm and the two of them stood together. He hadn't laughed at all, but he said,

I'm glad that we can laugh about it. Will you laugh about it with us?

I wasn't sure what they were asking. I nodded.

He took a picture down from the mantel, two boys standing by a fence. A peacock was in the background.

Which one is me? he asked.

My son has gotten lost on many occasions. Anytime we have gone somewhere crowded, he loves to do something and that thing that he loves to do is to wander off. When he has done so, it becomes impossible to find him again, for he is so overwhelmed with simply perceiving what can be seen in a crowd like that, at a fair like that, at a zoo like that, at such a circus, promenade, boardwalk, metropolitan train station, that he plays no part in being found. When he is again found it is clear that he was, if anything, working adamantly to not be found, but in an entirely passive way. By that I mean, he joins the scenery of the place, delighted to learn the things that he can learn there, making no effort to call attention to himself, and in this he is very practiced. Many a time, my wife and I could be seen scouring some place, with the aid of sometimes dozens of people, desperate to find him. Where then is he found? He is sitting in a shop window eating an ice cream cone with an old woman. Or he is riding in a flamingo boat with a family of Asian tourists. Or he is sitting on the ground, looking at the heaving sea of legs.

It is certainly true that at all times the world is fascinating. At all times all parts of the world are eternally fascinating. There is no legitimate rubric that could be used to choose the doing of one thing over the doing of any other. So when he chooses to simply observe this or that, and, I presume, leap out of his heart into some empathy with the thing observed, whether it is a Ferris wheel or a tortoise, I have never been capable of objecting, and certainly, I have never sought to change what is essentially to my eyes, a basic resourcefulness that finds at any moment something profound. My wife was of the same opinion, but surely we did suffer for it. The long apologies we would have to give to the legions of helpers. But strangely, no one was ever angry about it. People become fond of him very quickly, and that has always helped.

That we must mark the people who have been sub-
jected to the census is clear. How that mark should
look—so to speak, what it, in essence, is, is set down
by a mandate made in the place of the census bureau.
It is emblazoned in the eye of every census taker. Yet,
the manner in which the mark is given is absolutely
unclear.

Yes, it is a tattoo. But, how to create it? A census taker
showed me a sort of ink-gun, like a stapler, which is
laid upon the rib, and in one fell swoop stamps the
tattoo in its entirety upon flesh. Perhaps I am old fashioned, but I find this device hideous, and would never
use such a thing.

It could be that my background as a surgeon prepared
me for the work of tattooing. In fact, I do not mind it
at all, although I have never in truth done any tattoo
apart from the census mark.

For this work, I use a mechanical tattoo needle, and
fresh black ink, the method for the making of which I
have become acquainted with, in case it should ever
happen that I run out. The danger of blood contamina-
tion is gotten over by using fresh needles. I foresee difficulties in the future with this, as I cannot forever know
that I will have access to fresh needles. Therefore, I
have read a manual about older methods of tattooing,
if it should come to pass that I must set my mechanical
needle aside. To be completely honest, in some ways
I long for the simplification that would therefore take
place, as I have watched several films of the old Japa-
nese and Polynesian methods, and I find them very at-
tractive, although I understand in my heart that they
are painful, and would cause me no end of trouble.

»

Perhaps you wonder how it is that we managed to find a bed each night? The truth is—we often ended up sleeping in the car, and though it was winter, it was not so bad, for this car, which was made by a company called Stafford, long out of business, has a sort of built-in heater that can run when the car is off. It heats the front compartment only.

The car was an old taxi-cab, and the idea, I guess, was that it would save gasoline if the engine wasn't running while the taxi waited on cold nights for a fare. So, every now and then I fill the little stove with its own supply of fuel, and then during the night it goes on periodically, every fifteen minutes for a minute or two, just enough to keep us from freezing.

The vehicle was originally called the Carriagecar (one word), but it swiftly became known as the Stafford *manhandler*—the police used it as a paddy wagon. I bought ours from a used car dealer for almost nothing, with the intention that we would own a car that we didn't actually ever want to use, and that owning such a car would force us to walk or bicycle. My wife agreed about this proposition, and we never much used the automobile.

So, this trip was a moment of vivid life for the Stafford. Probably it had never managed to have much of a good time in the yard next to the house where we lived, and now it was just gobbling road, rolling its wheels on every sort of surface, braving rain and snow, skirting the edges of flooded streets. What a life!

When my son was young, my wife wrote a book for him in which the Stafford was a character. It became a sort of touchstone, and, as it turns out, was crucial in making him comfortable with the idea of this trip. Yes, we would be going far away to places we have never been. Yes, we might never come back. However, we will be in the Stafford Carriagecar. In that sense, everything will always continue to be just the same. Do you see that?

Two women lived in a house at the edge of F. We came on it from the outside, and so it was the first place we stopped. I wanted to pass it by, but my son insisted. Why did he insist? I think it was because there was a round window in the face of the house.

There was a bedraggled garden in the yard, and no clear driveway. I pulled up on the grass and we walked around the garden. I noticed the wreck of a squash and signs that other things too had failed to receive harvesting. The house was one of those false log cabins. What I mean is: the outside is made to look like it is built from logs, but of course it isn't. I have always saved a special hate for these houses.

When we knocked on the door, it was answered by a great deal of barking. After a time someone came—a woman dressed to go out, coat and all. The dogs pushed past us, and she did too.

What is it you want? Oh, knock again—my sister will come. And I will be back in a while.

She went away across the yard and down the road, smaller and smaller, smaller and smaller until the leash was too thin to be seen, and soon she was too.

We knocked again. This time a young woman came.

You can never trust my older sister, she told us, as we sat by a fire that she made before our very eyes.

I doubt that she will come back tonight. She hates strangers, and men, and strange men most of all. She dislikes travelers and old men, and old travelers. She doesn't like drivers, she doesn't like musicians, she doesn't like gypsies. Do you have a dog? She tolerates those, if they are hers, but yours would be yours, and so she probably wouldn't like it, not unless you gave it to her, which she would never accept, never.

Her sister was the famous comic writer G. Salter. It was through the money earned by the books that the two sisters lived, and so, of course, the younger sister was very grateful. As she put it, *I was put on this earth with no purpose in mind*, and so I am very lucky that another who can earn her way was put down at my side. I suppose I would just wander the streets as a prostitute if not for my sister. She laughed and said it again. I would just be a sort of hired girl in the street. Just pin my miniskirt up!

She looked at me suddenly, playing at being cautious. You're a little old for such things, though, aren't you?

She laughed again in the midst of her faux-caution.

I am so tired of everyone who lives in this town! If you were a young man, why, I would just take you into my room this minute. I would practically beat you to death with sex. But you are a bit old, aren't you?

She laughed and laughed.

I'm frankly surprised you don't use a cane. Should I get you one? I think we might have one here—and we have no need for it. Ha. You and me, I'll bet we couldn't sleep together if we tried, I mean, if we had to, absolutely had to. We would roll around in bed and nothing would happen, nothing at all. We'd be like two children at a sleepover. How pathetic! Do you know I believe the human race should end—that this should be the final generation? My sister agrees, too. I had myself spayed by a veterinarian when I was nine. She was fourteen. We just covered ourselves in animal skins and slunk into the vet's office. It changed the way I look at everything, that day in the vet's office. I tell you that so you know—neither one of us will ever have a child.

She laughed some more and put some wood on the fire.

I was at a loss to know what to say, so I said should we begin? and she agreed.

The matter of the census was attended to, and then the marking. This was a bit of a shock to her, for, as she put it:

I almost die whenever I am hurt even the slightest bit.

Afterwards she asked if we would stay the night. I said we really ought to go. She said we really should just stay—it was so late.

This stalemate was broken by the door opening.

I see you haven't gone, said the older sister. I have been waiting in the yard for you to leave for the last hour, but if you won't, you won't. Let's get done with this business.

She threw her coat over a chair. The dogs ran into some other room and couldn't be seen or heard anymore.

You are a census taker?

How did you know?

She snorted:

Each day I slap myself in the face and wait a moment then look in the mirror. If the red of the slap has gone, then I know the day will go well. But if the red remains, I know some pathetic thing will happen to me. In this case it is you, a census taker. You are the thing that is happening to us.

I said that it wasn't as bad as all that. Really, it was just a sort of formality.

It is the opposite of a formality, she said. It is a purposeful inquisition.

I agreed that it was just that.

She looked around and noticed that her sister had no shirt on.

So, that's the situation, huh? I leave you for an hour and you wrap your legs around the first men who come, never mind that they're old and foolish? How tired I am of looking after you—if only someone would come and carry you off forever. Maybe I'll put an advertisement in my next book, a kind of sweepstakes. Winner gets my tart of a sister for his/her own to do with as he/she will.

She narrowed her eyes. Her sister did not make any motion to put her shirt back on, but instead flounced her hair like a girl in an old book.

Shut up, you. You're being unfair—it's just the tattoo to show I've been counted. And you must have yours also if we must pin you down to do it. So we will both be sitting here with half our clothes hanging off us. How's that?

We stayed there for a few days, and actually never went into the town. It turned out that the sisters wrote their famous books together, as co-authors—and neither one was very serious about anything, not in the slightest. My son was very happy—he took the dogs on long walks, and we ate several fine meals. I told them stories about the census, and also about my wife—someone they as cultured people knew, someone they had a high regard for. But eventually it was time to go.

As we sat in the car, as I turned the ignition and prepared to depart, the older sister poked her head through the car window and told me:

there is a film we have, a film of your wife's performance. It is the only one I have seen. Do you know it?

I said I had seen a few. Which was it she spoke of?

This one is a stage with an enormous plate on it, a napkin, a spoon. There are giant pieces of silverware, a knife and fork, hovering overhead managed by spectacular mechanical arms. Your wife is dressed as some part of the supper, and she spends the performance eluding the cutlery as a monologue is read by a man through a bullhorn. Do you know the history of that piece?

I shook my head. Of course, I did know, but I liked hearing it told to me. When the person you love has died, any indication that they once lived is received gratefully, or alternately, you want to pretend that nothing good has ever taken place in the world. In this case, it was the former.

The sister continued, leaning against the car, there, almost standing in her overrun garden speaking to us so powerfully, and thinking not of that, but of a distant place and time, and probably, simultaneously, a faint overlay of the person she herself was when she first watched the film in a third time and a third place, and in that faint overlay some sense of dissonance—her understanding of the world at the time, and her present understanding now. Telling stories is a visitation of this sort—for the stamp bears the impression not just of what it was to begin with, but of its every use.

The sister continued:

She wrote it with another girl, and they both performed it, alternating nights. In a performance the week before the one they filmed, just a week before it, the other girl was crushed and killed by the fork: right in that same theater. No one had been coming to see the show, they were about to close, but once that happened, the audience was packed every night. *This is the show that killed a clown.* That's what everyone was saying to each other. It became a famous thing. Perhaps you know the story?

I said the film was called that, The Show That Killed A Clown.

I can never remember, she said, what the famous monologue is about, which is strange, because, well, monologues are what I do. At the time when I am watching the film the man's words as he shouts them through the bullhorn, they seem to me to be unobjectionable, maybe even funny. But, afterwards: nothing. I don't even know who the man was.

He was a drunk, I said, a thoroughly drunk person recruited from the street moments before each performance. But, as for the monologue, I don't remember it either. I don't know that I can even hear it. I just remember from that piece, I remember the part where . . .

Where the fork and knife start to play with her—where you feel they know they have killed before, and they are only too happy, only too happy to kill again. It is the part where you feel she doesn't know what she is doing on the stage—that she must have wandered there by accident.

Yes, it is this part I like best.

»

My son wanted to be the one to administer the census in the next village, some satellite of F. I told him he could do it, but that he would have to be prepared, as I always was, for refusals, cruelty, indifference. I explained all the awful things that could happen.

We came up with a simplified version that he would do. I was to be his assistant.

We went to the first house. A boy came to the door. This greeter went away and came back with a larger version of himself. The two escorted us into the kitchen where we sat at the kitchen table. The man repeatedly tried to meet my eyes, but I always looked down. My son's questions were met with some confusion. He would repeat each query many times (which is also what I often have to do), and he wrote the answers down in a large folio notebook. He is not proficient in writing, but likes to do what I think of as a sort of semblance of writing—so it was as if their answers were recorded in some inscrutable simulacrum of wavy lines. The man kept peering over to see what it was that was being written, but my son held the folio at an angle such that it could not be seen.

I administered the census mark to the man, and he had objections to this—somehow the gravity of the endeavor was not properly clear to him. At that point, I was forced to show him my proofs. He quieted down.

How did you like it? I asked my son after the fifth house, a particularly difficult visit. The people in the fifth house pretended not to understand my son at all. I was forced to interpret. To begin with, these were not gentle people. They were not nice to each other, they were not nice to us. Luckily, he did not feel he had done anything wrong. It was clear to him that giving the census was not easy.

Five visits in that town—and he felt it was enough. He asked me what it was we were trying to do. I said that this was a difficulty for me also. It is hard, I said, convincing someone else to do something the value of which you do not understand.

But, do I, I asked myself as we drove on, doubt the census itself? No, a thousand times, no. It is only my particular application of it, an application mired in confusion, the confusion of my life and circumstance. I imagine in my head, late at night, what a real census taker would be like, the manner of his arrival at a house, the greeting he would receive, what questions he would ask, caparisoned, as it were in garments of silver, moonlight perhaps?

That something beyond you longs to know your humble circumstances, longs to know every last detail of your feeble and utterly failed life: what does it mean?

I put the papers my son had written along with all the other papers and when we reached the next post office, mailed them together. There may be someone at the bureau who can see what I cannot—for whom something certain resides in places where my eye can only quiver and fail.

I think I first came upon the cormorant not in the open air but in the pages of a book—as a boy reading *Paradise Lost*. Satan costumes himself that way—and it is understandable, I think, for him to do it. We don't just pick costumes for their efficacy, but also because we delight in them, and like how we look. It is funny to me to think of Satan and the woman of San Nicolas Island wearing a similar garb, though I suppose Satan also had a beak and webbed feet, light bones, etcetera. The question of whether Satan inhabiting a form has in actuality the form itself, or just the appearance of that form is one that has never been argued to any sort of conclusion by theologians, though they have tried. A possible answer is that he does not in any way resemble a cormorant when he is in a cormorant disguise; however, looking at him, you feel you are looking at a cormorant. This line of thinking would make us to feel that the woman of San Nicolas Island, despite not having the beak and wings of Satan's cormorant, in some sense comes closer to true cormoranthood than does he.

The truth is—at the time I did not even know what a cormorant looked like, so knowing that Satan was disguised as a cormorant was to me knowing nothing. I had an idea that a cormorant was a kind of crow. Later I learned from Mutter that I was not alone in this belief—an entirely false one. The cormorant is no corvid cousin.

There is a theory about Milton, that he made Satan use a cormorant shape because that wondrous water bird is unskilled at flying. The cormorant's wings are too short to fly well. It can be argued that it almost— that it almost doesn't fly. In fact, the cormorant does fly, but it is tiring for it to do so. Of course the reason is—it must swim well, and graceful wings made for the air are no help in swimming. To me it makes sense that Milton might have wanted Satan to be a bit uneasy in the sky, as a kind of precautionary measure, a tinge of color, however, this is not entirely consonant with the fable of evil as we know it, for don't witches flee into the air at the slightest provocation? Wasn't Satan himself an angel?

»

Years ago a woman came to me with a puzzling condition. She was a friend of my wife's.

Can we have this conversation in confidence?

Yes, of course.

I am beginning to have trouble recognizing my husband.

What do you mean?

I mean—I can't recognize him anymore, if we are in a large group. If I have to meet him in public it is hopeless. I just stand there and wait for him to approach me and declare himself. It's all I can do.

If someone else were to do it, were to approach me as I stood there in the crowd—well, I would just go off with that person instead. I simply can't tell who he is.

The woman was about forty-five, a stage actress. She wore her hair in elaborate beehives and such, and always dressed in the finest clothing. My wife made endless of fun of her about it.

Her husband was an economist. The trouble was, as they grew in wealth, the two of them become more and more like everyone else, to the point that, as she said, she could no longer tell him apart from anyone. Presumably, the man himself was in the same difficulty—but he was too proud to seek help. Either that, or his philandering ways made it that he didn't care.

No, I am just joking about that. The mind weaves things this way and that. Actually, the sad truth was this: the woman, long a reluctant patient of mine, her husband had died earlier that year, and she refused to accept it. She would rather believe that she could no longer recognize him, that he had been lost that way, than to come to terms with his death.

I told her that the best thing for it was to find someone else, to find a person that she could both notice and identify, and to bind herself to him (or he to her). The disintegration of your marriage, I told her, is completed in anonymity, the anonymity in which no one can be told from any other. You must find someone remarkable.

This was very bad advice, and was prompted partly by the fact that I disliked the woman very much. I think it could be said that, if I believed she would take my advice, then the giving of that advice might be seen to be wrong. However, this woman had always despised me, and thought my opinions of no account. Therefore, the opinions that I gave her began to be of no account. Isn't that the spirit, the essence of fairness? Perhaps that is why some have said: there is no fairness in medicine.

In general, I have always avoided that realm of doctoring that touches upon the mind. I had a friend in medical school who was embarked that way. He became a great success, his speech a kind of cure-all, and I always felt that it was his ability to persuade people *against their will,* that made him successful. My wife hated him and wouldn't have him in the house.

That was a rule we had—no one could come to the house who was not universally loved (by myself, my wife, my son—that universe). We had few guests, obviously, but those few—how wonderful!

In the office of the census, I was given a sort of audition. I was there in the hopes that it would be a simple matter becoming a census taker. I was in a hurry, I was dying; is there any hurry greater than that?

Go out of the room, the census chief (local bureau chief) told me. Go out of the room, and come back in, and when you do, administer to me the census, as though to a stranger.

I went out, came back in, performed the first portion of the census, performed the second and the third, noted that I was near appropriate completion of the fourth (which does not always occur), made my appropriate completion, offered my goodbyes, and went out again. Then I waited.

I was told to come back in.

I went back in.

You are too formal, he said, and slapped his pant leg as if to knock dust off a glove.

You are too formal, he repeated, and you are also not formal enough. You prattle on when you should listen. You ask the questions as if the meaning of the question is obvious, rather than asking it in such a way that the person is removed past himself/herself to the place in which the answer resides. Are questions so obvious? I think not. Do not let yourself make them so.

When you ask a question you are not looking for the rote answer stored in the brain. Why, you could have that yourself without asking—save everyone the trouble. Instead, you are looking for a reconsideration of that question in light of the person's entire lived experience, something *you cannot know until you are told.*

Your body, your extended hand, the tautness of your face, the turn of your foot—it must all shout: I here and now give you permission to live an examined life, beginning now with this moment in which I ask you a question and you, poor soul, may examine your life in the light that it sheds. This is a part, just one small part, of the grace that the census offers.

Not, where were your parents born—but, what is the meaning of a national boundary? When your parents crossed such a thing to come here—how did it change them? Why did they do it? Who were those people who left the place that they came from—fearful, hopeful, full of a joy long since extinguished, perhaps replaced with fresh joy, perhaps not—who were they, and how, in all the wild mystery of earth and its citizens, could they have come to be the people now crushed by age, waiting fitfully in the waters of death's first sleep?

You begin by saying to me, hello—by greeting me, and yet, the greeting you give is a mere pleasantry, rather than a precursor, a spur, to actual experience. You must jolt the life of the person you face so that the matter at hand can come to light in a lived moment.

So many things wrong, so many. He shook his head.

When you look into my eyes as I am speaking, you make me lose my train of thought. If I begin to speak and the eyes are met, then leave them, and if I begin to speak and you are looking away, then look away.

You can only meet my eyes while I am speaking if I come to a rhetorical point—where I am asking in some sense if you pay attention. Otherwise this action of yours—to meet my eyes—only disturbs me by declaring (in meeting my eyes), I exist, and I am standing here. Does this profane waving of the envelope of the interaction serve any purpose? Perhaps if a person has wandered far afield in answering a question, perhaps then—but even so, perhaps not, for it is at such times that the census often comes upon what is most valuable.

Do you even know what the census is?

»

I confess to you, my audition for the census was in some ways completely humiliating. The chief reached for an illustrative example, he told me that a snide boy curling his lips into a sneer as he passed each house on his own street—that this would be of more service to the census than the pathetic performance he had witnessed. At least, he said, that would not discomfit the populace. They are used to that sort of thing already.

You must understand the basic position that you are in when you enter someone's house. You might well be the first person to ever enter that place. The man or woman you speak to might know no one. He or she might speak a language not heard in a hundred years. You must consider yourself a sort of archaeologist, a scientist, an artist, a priest. But you must add to those professions a strong dose of that immemorial office: the vagrant fool. You must truly see that you are of no account.

Why do you inquire? Why indeed? If faced with a question you cannot answer, do not ever try to answer it. Simply be patient, amass, amass. An answer might come—or a more particular question.

The census taker does not arrive as a child to a doll's house, all seeing, all comprehending. We do not pry off the roof to investigate. In fact, the situation is quite the opposite. It is we who have no freedom, we who are bound to a running wheel that moves on a fixed path a thousand miles to its end with nary a moment to breathe or smile.

Think rather that we are a scab on a dog's neck. The dog in its ignorance will, we are sure, attempt to scrape at us, to claw us off, but we must cling to it if we are to do any good.

I asked him to explain this. I did not understand—in this metaphor, the census is the scab and the dog is the nation?

He laughed at me.

What is our purpose? Is it the dog we are trying to help? Perhaps in some way—but in a more general, or more precise sense, you choose, it is the house that the dog guards—that is where the good we do is bound. The dog guards the house, we guard the wound upon the dog's neck.

He pointed to a painting on the wall, a painting of a dog in an uncomfortable posture beside a fence post. Upon close inspection, the dog could be seen to have a wound on his neck, a wound covered in scabs.

The census chief covered his mouth as if telling a secret:

An old manner of looking at it is to say that each census taker is a scab and each person is the dog, that the house is the nation, etcetera. In this sense, we are in the realm of synecdoche, for each scab is all scabs, each person is all people—humankind and scabkind respectively. This was thought for a time to be the right way of looking at things.

Now, on the other hand we go about it a different way. The census itself, at the moment given, is the scab, the wound is what isn't known about the populace—it is therefore not just in what manner the dog has been injured, but rather, in what manner the action of the defending of the house has been altered by the wound. Does the dog shy away? Does he whimper? Does he hide beside a fence post because he cannot do his duty? The census, in learning his capability, somehow ameliorates the situation by taking into account the dog's excellences, what is left to it to do, and understanding its deficiencies—which of its tasks it can no longer perform. The idea of the house as the nation is also a known fallacy. The census is a matter for humankind in general—past nations, which, after all, bloom here and there like flowers, each one to its own paltry epoch. That which we can know, and continue to know—it is not bound to the nation. Once that knowledge exists, it exists.

He patted me on the shoulder, go you unlucky scab. Do what good you can.

I used to do exercises to keep my strength, but I have abandoned them for the duration of this trip. The reason is not that I know I will die soon, because I feel people should keep on with the routines they love, whatever the case. The reason: I feel that driving the Stafford is itself exercise. The car has almost no suspension to speak of, and bounces every which way. Driving the Stafford over rough and rocky roads is in effect the experience of being yourself dragged over those same roads—and at a fast clip! This was the experience of being a tinker, I suppose, long ago—traveling from town to town with clattering wares. Our wares (the census and its documents) have no sound, though—just the inchoate shape of lives, and so they cannot clatter.

My son would like very much to drive, but I do not let him. One day, though, as we went our way, we came upon a broad cleared space—the site of a fair to be, or a fair that was. So, I let him drive about there. He just handled the wheel, but it was quite thrilling for him. And, in watching, I once again felt the strangeness of driving—of piloting such an absolutely large object around with nothing whatsoever to stop me!

There were some metal uprights here and there that needed to be avoided, and it was never clear that he would avoid them—though he did. We drove quite slowly, just fifteen miles an hour or so, but it felt very fast, and as we went we sang at the top of our lungs. He would swing the wheel back and forth wildly, nearly tipping the car at times—it is not meant for such things. Two large birds were resting in the distance, on a fence and I could see their puzzlement, even though their faces weren't clear. Don't you ever feel you can look into an animal's face just as you would a person's?

When we had gone around again, I looked for them, but they were nowhere to be found.

My son said to me about the driving of the car, he said this after driving the car: now I am a driver. I said, yes, but don't drive the car without me. He said you don't drive the car without me.

»

It is fine to talk about exercises—but those are a matter for someone looking through the trees to the open air. I deceive myself when I pretend to that state of affairs.

For me, things were worse. I had felt it for a time, just as I had at home, a trouble, a tightening in my chest, and it had come more and more. Of course, I did not worry for myself, as I would have in many ways liked to be already dead, but for my son. His life is such that he is assured of nothing that continues. He needs a champion.

In G, I woke up and I was lying on the floor of someone's living room. My son was crying and holding my foot. A doctor was looking down at me, his face and five or six others. The faces were very close to me. People always come closer to an injured person than they usually would, as if the injured person takes up less space. That or they shun you.

What could I remember? I know I entered the house, I know I had begun to speak to them of the census, and then—I don't know.

The doctor got me to my feet after a while.

We spoke; he found he could extend a great courtesy: he took us back to his own home. He allowed us to stay there several days. He himself ministered to me daily. Why he would be so kind is hard to say. There are expressions, *some people are like that* or *it was the right thing to do.* I think it is more often simply luck. I must have reminded him of someone.

In any case, on the fourth day my condition passed, but I was very weak. I felt I should sit for another day or two, and he concurred.

I will give you a description of this man.

The man was about thirty, and eager to speak with me about all things medical. He would describe professional troubles, problems of this sort or that, and I would speak to them with my long experience. In the evenings, we played chess. He liked to think over his moves for a long time, both the obvious ones and the difficult.

I came here, he said, by a process of elimination. I didn't want to go to any of the places that I knew, I didn't want to practice there where I had been, anywhere I had been. So I went to a place that I did not know, thinking it might be different. But it is much the same. It is much the same, don't you think?

He said he had been there six years, and would probably never leave. The people who lived in G were easy to deal with, on the whole kind and well meaning. They liked him well enough, and respected him. There was a certain distance, a certain reserve displayed by almost everyone on account of his being an outsider, but he understood that. He was working on a medical dictionary, and constantly corresponding with other doctors all over the country. But it was good, he said, to be face to face with another like him, if I didn't mind him saying that.

I said I didn't mind at all. But, he should know that I was no longer a surgeon.

The profession is the profession, he said. You can't give it up, even if you want to.

I said there was one way to give it up for good.

He was very concerned about my heart, and gave me several medications. There are things that could be done, he said, certain drastic things. But he could see I wouldn't pursue those, and if so, if I wouldn't pursue those, well, then I knew already, most likely I knew, I must already know what he knew, which was that, if I was not at the end, I was at least very near it.

What will you do with your son? What will he do when you die?

There is someone he can go to—someone we know. I will send him back on the train.

That will be hard. Do you think he can travel alone?

He can do it. There is always someone who has it in themselves to help him. It is not a fact I have ever seen fit to rely on before, but it has always been true.

Do you ever wonder, the young doctor asked me, who he thinks he is? Who does your son think he is? I have a sense of myself and I'm sure you have a sense of yourself, and in some ways we attempt to obtain from others a recognition of it. I attempt in meeting you to ensure that you see who I think I am when you look at me. You do the same. But he does not appear to try very hard to do that. And so I wonder—who does he think he is?

I said that this is something my wife talked about, something she would bring up from time to time. One day, there was a box of photographs from our lives together, and she brought them all out. She and he went into his room with the photographs and he chose several to put on the wall of his room beside the door. He puzzled over them for hours, taking one down, putting another up. This became a kind of activity that would happen that summer, and I believe by the time the fall came, he had finished. The wall had reached a kind of solvency. From then on it did not change.

The fact that he chose the images for the wall, and that he liked to look at them did not really imply that he thought the person in the photographs was himself. And, in fact, I think we as people make a kind of mistake in believing this to be true in general about photographs of ourselves. Is that really you in the photograph? Or is it someone you have a connection with? Someone you once knew, but who now is foreign to you? A person whose concerns you share in part—but who is lost and gone away?

Because of this we did not insist with him that the photographs were him, although we often implied it. For some this may be an overly subtle point, but if you are not interested in such subtleties, then you will unwittingly forfeit many of the finest things that life gives to you to feel.

»

The photographs were attached to the wall with small black nails. My wife had a ball-peen hammer and she enjoyed using it for tasks that often deserved a real hammer. I am not even sure what a ball-peen hammer is for, or why she came to own one, but I imagine it was simply the innate oddness of the ball-peen hammer that drew her to it.

I heard the nails going in, one by one that first day. Then on days that followed all through the summer, my wife would be called up to the room to rearrange them, or to take one photograph down and replace it with another. We came to be very familiar with those photographs.

The first series, that ran highest on the wall, at his head height, were of a snow scene. I don't remember what year it was, though I think the year was written on the back of one or two of them. We had bundled him up in his winter clothes, and taken him sledding. Someone had given us an old fashioned sled—one that didn't work very well—and we had gone out to the yard to drag him around in it. This was his first real experience with snow—and he thought it marvelous. He climbed out of the sled and rolled back and forth in it, getting snow all over his face and nose. Then he began to cry and then he stopped, for he was happy. He ate some of the snow. He called out to us, some syllable—I guess it was a word for snow. He had a parka on, one with a big hood, and my wife and I took photographs holding him to commemorate the moment. First, one in which she hid behind him, holding him up. This was often her posture, to pretend to be doing something useful, while, in fact, concealing herself.

His expression as I hold him is rootless—he does not know that he is being photographed, and thinks that his mother is standing to have a look at him. But why?

She calls to him; in the next picture he breaks into a smile. I am beaming. What can she have said?

On the wall these two are separated with another where she and he look for something on the sled. From the shadows I think it must be late afternoon—and this leads me to wonder, what did we do all morning as the snow was falling? It is something I have forgotten. A thing was given to me—a marvelous morning with snow falling, a lovely wife and child, an afternoon to come out in the landscape—and I allowed it to pass in such a way that I can no longer feel it. What things did my wife say to me? What observations did I make that I hoped to think on again? All lost—but pointed at like an arrow by the late afternoon shadow cast by the sled in this photograph I no longer possess.

»

The next picture was of my son in a sink. He is of that size that he can bathe in a sink, and so, of course, we bathed him there. I understand that there are people who bathe small children in baths, but as far as we were concerned, the essential ridiculousness and joy of bathing a small human in a sink was not to be avoided or lost. This photograph recommends itself to my memory because of one thing—my son asked where the boy in the photograph was. Where is he? I asked him: when did he mean? In the picture the boy is in our house, the house we lived in, this house, this very one that we live in still, so I told him. And that is still where the boy is, but now the house is much smaller, much more familiar.

My wife would sometimes use the photographs to illustrate points that she was making, as she knew he knew them so well. She would say, and now we are going to work on this the way we worked on walking, do you remember how we worked on walking? And she would show him the picture in which she stands behind him holding his arms, as he steps forward on uncertain feet. Then they would return to the exercise, whatever it was, working on words, or letters, or singing, whatever.

Two photographs that were among the very first put on the wall, but that disappeared for months only to be put up at the last, the very last two, but set right in the middle of the proceedings, they were a pair of photographs of a raincoat, with him in it. There is a raincoat and a bannister and a boy in the coat, and I am in the shadows behind. In the next the hood of the raincoat is up and it has begun to appear to be the costume of a clown. I think this is why he liked the photograph. When my wife and he first saw it, she said, oh look, here you are a clown, like me. Here you are like me. Then something threw it out of favor and it disappeared into the pile only to be brought back again at the last, as a tie between mother and son. In truth, I think the photograph gives the impression of a clown not because of anything that is funny or comedic, but because there is a formality and gravity to the costume that has no bearing. It is this powerful expression of some specific place in a hierarchy that does not exist that is the wonder of a clownish costume— the regular elements of garments distorted, missized, deformed. Yet there is a freedom granted by that—and the freedom is, one cannot misuse the garment of a clown. Whatever one does is right.

On the back of the door, my wife put a photograph of our laundry line. She told him that the photographs he was choosing were like the laundry on the line and that he could place them however he liked, just as the laundry was placed, and that they could be fetched and returned and moved about in all the same ways, and even worn, pinned to a shirt, if he wanted.

»

The young doctor inquired: when did he learn about the camera—when did he know what it did? Did he learn to operate it himself?

I said he did not want to use the camera, who knows why. But he liked very much to carry it, and often did, and when it would come time to use it he would give it to my wife or to me, and the photographs would be taken. Though by that time, I think we took far fewer photographs, perhaps more out of a sense of obligation than anything else, though obligation to whom, I can't say.

My wife loved to take photographs of trees, and even more than trees, of the woods, of that grouping—no single tree, but conglomerations of branches. There was a photograph there on my son's wall where he stands with me and he grips my arm with his hand, and behind us there is a kind of wilderness of branches. It is my feeling that the photographer looked past us as she took the photograph, and that we are in it in some sense, only by chance. Still it was my favorite of the photographs that I was in, perhaps because of the position of the hat I was wearing, which is lowered over my eyes. This was my favorite hat for many years, and I lost it climbing. My wife and son would laugh at me when I spoke about any new hat that I owned but disliked, and there was a kind of joke my son would make where he would without breaking into a smile tell me that he knew very well where my hat was, it was upstairs, and I would play along and say, yes, if it is upstairs, why don't we go and get it, and he would say all right, and then up we would go, up the stairs, and I would say, well, you have me upstairs, where now, and he would lead me to his room, and I would say, is my old hat in your room, my old hat that I lost while climbing?, and he would nod, and lead me in, and then I would make a great display and demand that my hat be returned to me, and he would point with glee to the photograph and tell me if I wanted it, I could have it.

»

There is another boy who is in three of the pictures. He lived across the way, and his parents were not friendly to us. I believe the father hated us, there was some misunderstanding. But when the boy was young he would come often to play with my son. This went on for a year or more, and then one day, no more. They continued to live across the street, but would have nothing to do with us.

My son liked this boy very much, and so three pictures on the wall are photographs of him. I must say, in all honesty, this was a very bad boy. He would never listen and would always break things. Anything given to him was as good as broken. But we did not mind that, not very much, and treated him well until it came time for him to disappear into his own life.

They had a large dog, too, named Robber and when the boys were young, they would hold on to Robber's neck and be pulled about the yard.

I think the boy came most one year when the weather was very hot, because the impression I have from those photographs, and in general, in thinking of him, is one of intense heat. We made a lemonade stand for them, but no one came. It was a rather lonely road. I had to pretend to be a customer myself, but the boys were not deceived, and I know that they felt in their hearts it was not valid, although they gave me lemonade and charged me the agreed price.

Sometimes he would ask me, my son would ask why it was so dark in the photographs. I believe it is true that many of the photographs that we took were taken inside, and it is also true that the lens of the camera we owned was a rather poor one, and so the light was not good enough for excellent photography. Yet, two of the pictures that he liked the most, two that he did in fact refer to as being photographs of himself, were very dark pictures. In these two he is by a window, and wearing a striped shirt. His mischief is in his face, beneath the surface in the first, and fully apparent, covering his face, in the second, in which he has left the window, and is in motion towards us.

The last photograph, lowest on the wall, was of the garage outside our house. He is standing on the cracked pavement, and wearing a sport coat. I believe it was a first day of school, some first day of school, and he had gotten his clothing together in an official sense. He had prepared himself, and he wanted the moment commemorated. I think this because there is a set to his shoulders in the photograph that implies some kind of patience, or some bowing before the inevitable. Not that he was very resigned—as a child he was not one to be resigned to things. If anything he was a mule.

He does not seem so stubborn to me now, said the doctor. Why he is very courteous.

We looked over at my son, who was asleep, curled on a couch.

Look he has even removed his shoes before putting his feet up on the sofa.

Oh he is thoughtful, I said. But the thoughtful ones are often the most stubborn, don't you think, when they have a sense of justice, of injustice?

The doctor collected old books and he showed us many beautiful medical atlases, many tomes of curiosities. He seemed to enjoy showing them to us, and his voice became very warm as he spoke.

The naming of things has never been systematic, he said—this was his chief complaint. It makes the body an impossible morass, but it need not be so. He proposed an entire new scheme of naming—the renaming not just of every part of the body, but also of all illnesses, so that the entire matter of the human form and its sicknesses could be easily understood.

I said there was one difficulty—that we could at this moment only come up with a scheme of naming as perfect as our present understanding of the body. That, in effect, a dozen or two dozen years from now, the state of medical knowledge would have moved forward, and that it would become necessary to, in essence, do the very same thing once more, renaming everything in order to fit a new and more profound consensus.

Of course, of course, he agreed. His feeling was that this should happen once every fifty years.

»

I went about with him in the last days of my recovery and found him to be an excellent practitioner. He would introduce me as a senior colleague, despite my dress, and would solicit my opinions as he dealt with matters of all kinds. Only once did he truly need it, as I recognized the presence of a special sort of cyst that he had never seen, but that I had often dealt with. We talked the procedure over thoroughly the night before my son and I left.

Won't you stay? Perform the operation, or even just assist?

It is within you to do it. Certainly it is.

He had an immense fear of seeing his own blood, strange in a doctor, and he would not for anything be marked by the census needle. He had the mark of the previous census, though. How? I asked.

I was holding a friend's hand and I fainted dead away, he said with a laugh. The room disappeared before my eyes, and it has been replaced with this.

He gestured to his books, statues, leather-clad desk, his carpeted study.

I feel so old, right now, he laughed. Don't you always find you are the age of the person you are talking to? I feel, I feel speaking to you that we have lived together your life of surgery—so many years of life. And, I suppose you feel, speaking to me, that you are a young man, just beginning his practice. You can feel what I feel in that regard. But the years will pass quickly. Soon, I, like you, will be near the door.

The body gets used up, but the mind continues, like a darting bird, I said quietly.

A darting bird, wingless in the open air.

We laughed together. My son laughed too.

It was time to leave. It could be delayed no further. The doctor came out with us to the car and stood waving as we went, as we approached the distance, at which point he vanished completely, he and the town of G.

Mostly as we drove, my son and I talked about things we had spoken of many times before, things that we both knew about, and liked to talk about. It wasn't necessary to talk about new things very often, or I should say, only if they really merited it.

One of the old things that came up again and again was The Shape School. It is the school where my wife went to live when she was ten. Such a place! The Shape School was an experimental school. The idea was that it would serve the ordinary purpose of education for ordinary students, but in an extraordinary way. In fact, what it did was turn out clowns.

There is a shape to everything, so it was said by the teacher at The Shape School, herself a famous mime. If you can enter into and assume the shape of something, then you can demonstrate it to someone else. You must become a library of shapes.

I believe there were two teachers and perhaps forty students during the decade in which The Shape School was in operation. Like clowns, the teachers could not keep their hand on the tiller for longer than that. They wandered off to other pursuits.

The Shape School was housed in a military barracks that had been disused for a decade before coming on the market. I suppose that's when the clowns found it and thought—how funny would it be to have a clown school in an army barracks. Though, of course, they didn't think of it as a clown school. In fact, as I said, it was quite the contrary: they had genuine pedagogical aspirations to perform only the most basic work of education.

But, for the time that it existed—I think no one would have wished to be anywhere else. I suppose that isn't entirely true, as of the total population through the years of forty students, they ended up with only six graduates. But a school of that sort must be hard—if only to challenge its finest pupils, who in this case, were those that no one else would ever have raised up or lionized. The finest pupils of The Shape School would have been degenerates and laughingstocks in any other school.

My son liked for me to tell the story of the boating lesson. It was announced one morning to the students, to the first class, some fifteen pupils, that they would learn to go boating. Everyone was instructed to wear a bathing suit and to bring nothing of value. Children are always squirreling away precious things in their pants, socks, sleeves—and so this was a wise precaution.

The group went down to the lake, where there were two rowboats. The instructors took one, and rowed out a ways.

With a bullhorn they yelled out—and their voices were clear over the plane of water, come on now, come on. Let us see which two can have the best accident.

So all day they were at it, the students going two by two out onto the lake, and failing at boating in one way or another, ending up spluttering and coughing, dragged by the neck or shirt or arm out of the cold lakewater.

There is a proper way, the older instructor said, to have a boating accident. We will demonstrate.

The instructors then set out to boat, and were overcome by a complete catastrophe that saw the rowboat overturned, an oar broken, and one of the two instructors not found for a good twenty minutes, at which time she emerged from the bushes on the far side of the lake.

That is how to have a boating accident.

For, as they said, it is not just about the truth of the thing, but that there is some common essence to the accidental, and that you must not simply have your accident pervaded with the essence of itself, but that essence must, in some sense, be magnified. Its essential nature as accident must be signal, must be obvious to the onlooker in a direct way—it must call to the person within the onlooker, she who has fallen from a boat, perhaps ten years ago, skipping over all the days and things that have come to pass since, and leaving her in an abject state of empathy, of total understanding. At that point it is even possible to remove the boat accident itself. For instance . . .

At this point, the instructor performed a boat accident, but not in the lake. She performed it there on dry ground with only her hands and feet to help her, and astonishment was general through the crowd. For, just as on the water, a calamity had come, and it was clear, as clear as day, that it had not come from within the mime, but from without.

Where then does it come from?

My son always wanted to know where the instructor went when no one knew where she was—when the boat had overturned and the oar had broken. He, my wife and I, we would try to analyze it: did she swim underwater the whole way? Was she ever in the boat? These were the questions. My wife, who, of course, had been the one to first tell the story to us, she said the instructor was in the boat and that she had swum the distance holding her breath. But then there was a reservation about this. For it to seem a proper accident, wouldn't it be impossible to get a deep breath while the boat overturned? Wouldn't that ruin the idea of the accident (if you were overseen)? Everyone agreed that it must have been a very stealthy breath. Because it isn't like a magician's trick—you can't know where the audience will be looking when you have a boat accident. They may well be looking straight at your face, and if so, then you had better not be taking a deep breath just before it happens.

The alternate theory—that only one instructor was in the boat, is conceivable. One instructor rows out, has the boat accident, and then asks where the other is, and states that she was in the boat, too. The human mind will supply a second instructor in the boat. Sadly, it is the case that we are this fallible and credulous.

To this idea, my son said, she would want to be in the boat. They want to be in the boat together.

Although, there are many objections to this statement, there is something essentially right about it. The lens is set at the right distance, and that is: the instructors are just people like anyone else. Given the opportunity to be in an overturning boat, they will take it, regardless of this frame of teaching. We have all had an experience of this kind, when we are hiding and watching a group of people who begin to do something that we would like to join in. Yet, we must keep to our contract, we must continue to hide, and it tears us almost in half—our desire to join in the delight of whatever pastime it is, whatever treat is being shared, and our firm intention to remain hidden.

One can take this as a sort of principle, so my wife told me—that we must be positioned within our deceptions in such a way that we can be afforded the maximum continued delight. It is useless to be Atlas.

As we drove on, a feeling grew in me. It has always been my opinion that if you are performing an operation of any sort, not a medical operation, I don't mean that, although certainly, that too is an operation, and what I say now applies also there, but I mean, more generally, any sort of operation whatsoever—if you are engaged upon a pursuit that you will assay again and again, then you should change up the manner in which you do it, you should experiment in small ways in order to be assured that you are in fact performing it in the best way possible. Too often people permit tradition to stand in for misunderstanding, or vice versa, and then the mistakes that were made in comprehension are compounded, mistakes that are, in many cases, correctable with logic alone. Think then of what the careful pursuit of excellence can do, giving no heed to anything but what functions—it was this way with me regarding the census.

I felt suddenly that the census taking we had done already was of a particular kind, and that we needed no longer to do it in that way. I was sure: I could use what I knew now about census taking to begin a new method of performing the work, a method that would adhere in a fundamental way to the spirit of the census, but that would permit my human fallacy less rein in its ruinous deceits.

NEW METHOD OF THE CENSUS

The new method of the census was an objection to the formal aspects of the previous method. Where before it was seen to be necessary to ask specific questions, and thus to privilege the gathering of certain information over other information, now it became clear that we could decide what information to look for. To have the luxury of subordinating oneself to one's superiors, certainly it is a delight. In an immediate sense, one is never other than a lectured child at such times, and one finds what one is asked to find, if one finds anything at all. However, out in the world I have come to see that he who looks too hard for any particular thing, though he may find it, will certainly miss the most wondrous and strange things he passes, though they stare him in the face.

So the typical work of the census, then, I abdicated. Other census takers, more literal minded than myself, perhaps would come to know the precise population of these regions. I, who have in some ways always misbehaved, even as a surgeon, would misbehave going forward, I decided. I would go into each house and home, each town and village, and try to discover what was worthy of note.

I realize in a way that it is vaguely ridiculous, no, just plainly ridiculous, for me to behave as though this were some new method. In fact, travelers of the past, Herodotus, Tacitus, Marco Polo, behaved in just this fashion. So, those were the sandals in which we marched on.

Although, it should be said—we are not looking for any of the things those legendary danger-seekers looked for. We prefer the small, the overlooked. This is not the same world into which they were born.

What is it Herbert says about the world we live in, a world in which the divine is not on any map?

But now thou dost thyself immure and close in some one corner of a chambered heart.

Isn't that what he said? Our census will look there . . .

The next town was known for its rope factory. In this place was made the very largest and strongest rope, rope used to tie ships to docks and anchors, rope for the lifting of impossibly heavy things through the air. Other ropes were made too, slender and smooth ropes, harsh and frictive ropes, wet ropes, spiced ropes, even strings and twines.

The foreman at the rope factory made an interesting statement in my presence. He said, there have been no accidents today.

Ah, no accident, not today.

No.

Is it often the case that there are accidents?

We walked to a chart placed on the wall. It detailed the history of accidents at the factory in the ten year period previous.

Mostly six per day.

Bad accidents?

We keep a doctor on hand, so they don't usually die, but it does change a person to be struck by a breaking rope.

Does the doctor have a moment to speak with us?

»

The doctor had a moment to speak to us, and so he did.

The doctor had a face like a leading man, and he spoke his lines like an actor.

The doctor wore a very white coat, as doctors often do, but this coat was even more white than that. It was whiter even than I say here.

The doctor acknowledged us with what I can perhaps call a speech—one he must have been waiting some years to give. Or perhaps it was extemporaneous; it is so hard to know these things. He was going to tell us about the rope factory, and so he did, and in a manner perfectly fitting his person and position.

He began,

The power of a bowstring has in times past been sufficient to kill a man at a distance of several hundred meters. What then a rope a thousand times as thick? The floor of the rope factory is knee deep in the blood that has been shed here. I hate this place, I hate the rope itself. I work here only because my father did, and my grandfather, my mother and my grandmother. Every one of them lost their lives here. So I went to the army and learned to be a medic, and then when I returned I went to medical school and learned to be a doctor, and then I avoided any lucrative employment and came here, where I work without pay helping these terrible fools.

We looked out through the broad window of the sickroom onto the factory floor. It was crisscrossed with thousands of ropes, ropes so long they could encircle the earth any number of times. Machines whirled this way and that, the sound was like clock-sound, but bent by tremendous whirring, like a dopplered clock flung past you and returned, flung past you and returned, but continuous, each tick, each tock, somehow stretched. It was a wild sound—I say finally it was like the gnashing of teeth.

Here and there small figures ran back and forth beneath the great ropes, some carrying implements, some pulling carts of one sort or another. Others stood in groups awaiting instructions. Their uniforms bore many different colors.

I asked the doctor about it.

It is important to know if anyone is out of place. Everyone in the factory must stay in particular areas, and keep their feet fixed to exact corridors.

The floor of the factory was covered with just such delineated paths, in varied paints.

Is it the case that the people who come here maimed, the victims, that they have been where they weren't supposed to be?

Behind me, one of the patients started to object.

The doctor hushed him. He had a sort of priestly power over everyone in the infirmary. His expression as he turned to me was harsh.

On the contrary, as you yourself say, they are *victims*. The workers take their daily endeavors so seriously that almost no one is ever out of place. In fact, it is true that the working of the machines takes into account *a necessary recklessness*. That is to say, the rope machines cannot be operated safely. It is impossible for any factory on earth to safely make rope. Behind the factory, if you should go there, you will find a field of poles. On each pole there is a knot in glass. This is the cemetery for the factory workers. When they take their breaks, when they eat their half-day rations, it is there that they do it. It is an old custom, designed to remind them of how close death is—how certain. I thought when I was a boy that I would work in the rope factory. I was certain of it. In fact, it was a matter of pride. I wanted nothing more than that. But, my father anticipated me. He took me out back of the house one day, and using a cigar cutter he did this.

The doctor showed me his hands. Where the thumbs should be there were two pale rounded bumps.

He touched the bump of one absent thumb with his forefinger. You see, I will never make rope. Never. At the time, a few other families did the same—and it was this action, that led to some of the conditions improving at the factory. At the time, at the time things had gone too far.

Several of the patients had come and were huddled around us listening.

But how can you do the work of a doctor? I asked. Doesn't it make it difficult?

The doctor looked down at his charges as if pondering my question, but when he turned to me, it was as if he had forgotten me. The work of a doctor? This work?

He said tersely, bending each word like a thread, oh it is no trouble. No trouble at all.

»

We went out, my son and I, behind the factory, and it was true. It was just as the doctor had said. There was a field, near as large as the factory, which is to say, almost the size of a town, stretching away and away. The factory is on an immense hill, the kind of hill that they used to fight battles on, a hill you could line two armies up facing. It is a hill for generals, and for days that will not be forgotten, but are always forgotten, and maybe should be. The factory took up the heights, stretched across them for a mile. Beyond it, down the hill, the cemetery reached. It was so large that no one could possibly keep it as cemeteries are kept. That is to say, there was not grass between the graves, but wild plants of every kind, and if there was grass, it was only by chance and not design. These plants and trees provided an antidote to the unceasing stand of grave poles—which did, as the doctor said, each bear a glass knot of rope. There were more trees and more trees and even undergrowth as the slope proceeded. We walked all the way down, jumping here and there like goats, and we noticed as we went, that the manner of the glass knots changed, and when eventually we reached a point, it must have been three or four miles down, where the knots became stone knots on dirty rusted poles, then from there we could see the outskirts of the next town, some miles off through a thin wood, downhill all the way. I became horribly winded at some point and had to stop and lie down on my back between the overgrown graves. My son thought I was playing and ran off, and it was an hour before I found him, much further on. Eventually, we came through a break of woods to a road, and down that road to a larger road. We'd left the Stafford outside the factory—but after a while we found someone to drive us back to it, some kind soul. The driver's face is lost to me already. How shocking it is to feel how little one can care, in receiving a kindness. I should remember such a face, but I do not. Perhaps my son does.

One thing nagged at me. I kept wondering as we went, why did the cemetery begin so far from the factory? Shouldn't it have been the other way? The oldest graves should be beside it. How can such a thing be done backwards? It was a sort of puzzle, and plagued me all the way.

»

suppose the walk was a mistake—an overreach. I spent the next days in a rented room being fed soup by a kindly old couple. They ran a shop and lived above it. I believe they rented the room once in a while when travelers came through, though it didn't look to me like it had seen much use. The shop was a milliner's shop on one side and a general store on the other. I don't know how many women's hats you can possibly sell in a town like that. I expect most of their business came from the general store. While I was abed, my son helped out in the shop. They took to him immediately, and knew just the sorts of things he might want to do. When he likes how things are going, he often becomes quiet about them, and he was this way about his work in the shop.

I couldn't figure out why they were so kind—not that people need a reason. But many people do have one, and it can pay to look for it, although as they say, it never pays to look too hard. From the moment that we arrived, quite late at night, possibly even waking them up with our knocking (to inquire about the rented room sign above the door), they received us with a gentleness of manner that was unforeseeable.

Two days later, as I sat by the window of that little room, a room decorated for the most part with nautical pictures, although there was a scythe upon one wall, doubtless to scare off the specter of death with his own armament, the woman sat in a chair across from me. She had given me my bowl of soup, and always before it had been her habit to retire immediately. But now she stayed. She sat down in the chair opposite and put both her hands flat on the table.

I want to tell you something, she said. My daughter was like your son. She is dead now for many years. But we raised her and she lived here with us, and joined with us in all the things that we did. She liked to sew things, although it was not easy for her, and she liked surprising people. She did not like to be surprised, but no one does. I wanted to tell you about her, because I think there are so few people in these later days who care about the kind of person they are. It even happens that no one has them anymore. I can see from the way you are with him that you see—you see what we saw, that they experience the world just as we do, and maybe even, maybe even in a clearer light.

I wanted you to know, she said, because there is so little support for this way of thinking. My husband said you knew already, and I needn't say anything. But, I wanted to. For people to see you two traveling together, and to see how your son can live and take joy—I think you cannot know the good you do. We weren't travelers like you, we didn't go that far in showing her the world, but at least we didn't keep our daughter in our home out of sight. In the mornings she would go out and wander the town, and everyone knew her. There is a kind of understanding that can grow in a place, and then everyone, every last person can be a sort of protector for them. This is a thing she can confer on others—a kind of momentary vocation, and it is a real gift. In large cities, other places, I know, people can be cruel. Some people were cruel to her, but here, something grew. It was a fine place for her to live, and when she died, she was missed.

The woman stood up. I looked at her.

The woman went away out of the room and I sat breathing, just breathing until the light left the window.

Mutter writes about naming that a name is almost always a sort of cowardice—an attempt to confine a thing to being only what it is, rather than what it may be. The progeny of a cormorant cannot still be a cormorant, she writes—at what point does it change enough to be accounted a new species? Who is wise enough to know this? Does this change happen in a generation—between a mother and a daughter, a father and a son? She disliked immensely a name sometimes used for cormorants, shag. The truth is, she didn't care for the cormorant varieties that go under that title, liking least of all those with crests.

In reading her works, one begins to suspect that she must have had an unfortunate experience at one time or another with a crested thing, whether a bird, a helmet or a hill—for her vitriol knew no end.

I mention this all because the census is a document that does not care about names. You may have any name or any other name and the census does not know. We merely obtain our precious knowledge from you, we merely mark you so that you will not give it twice, and then we merely go on our way, merely that. We merely do that, and we need not know your name at all.

It seems to me that there is an excellence in discrimination—in telling one thing apart from another, in being able to break a thing down into parts and see it simultaneously as its parts, and as a whole—and to do this for all things that one sees, to be simultaneously examining both grain and branch, to see the pore the limb the leap all together. But this endeavor is often tied to another—that is, that each part should be named. The naming of each part, and the knowing of these names is then spoken of as being identical to the excellence of discriminating between the parts. In fact, it is useful only in so much as one might choose to speak about any particular part. The wondrousness of felt experience resides in the discrimination, not in the name.

So I would be speaking for, then, a world without names—wherein we see what is, and are impressed by it—the impressions push into us and change us forever. This is the world I believe my son lives in.

But for myself, on the other hand, I do love names, and collect them. I like those old thoughts—that names have power; but, even more, I simply like to say names. The naming schemes that run with this language or that—unfathomable to me, can nonetheless be seen and heard to be intensely beautiful. I like nothing better than to see a list of names, or to hear a name said.

Can we not feel two opposite things at once? To whom is it a crime?

»

The notion that a person may influence another without speaking is an ancient one. *All flesh is continuous.* This was the iteration of that idea voiced at The Shape School.

The students would be given feelings—joy, surprise, anger, and be asked to convey those feelings to another student, who was under the burden of doing nothing at all. The second student, as an audience, should not work to oppose what was being done, should not be stoic, but beyond such proscriptions, the task was simply to sit and be a person and feel. Then the first student would come and try to have the second student feel exactly the anger she was feeling.

A barrier to this is that commonly the bridge of emotion from one to another is not a mirror. This is to say—if a person is angry, sometimes it makes you afraid, or if a person is afraid sometimes it makes you angry, or even delighted. If a person is sad, sometimes it disgusts you. One can't just be an emotion and expect it to do the work for you. Certainly, a crowd can have the effect of conveying its emotion to a singleton placed upon its edge. A crowd of terrified people is terrifying. I'm sure everyone has felt this. In the same way, a crowd of angry people, if you do not feel you are the prey of this anger, is angry-making. You can easily join in the anger.

So, in some sense, then, we have a beginning there: the person who wants to send her emotion to someone else must somehow obtain for herself the plurality of a mob, which can perhaps be seen to be one of two things: either that she appears as if in numbers, or that the person she is entreating can be made to feel absolutely small. The latter is not something that would have been acceptable to the proprietresses of The Shape School, as their principles stood against trivializing the lives or injuring the spirits of their audience members, so it left only the former. How then to become a crowd by oneself?

How indeed?

»

The measures and manner of tutelage of The Shape School turned out to be of great use to my wife when it came to pass that my son was born. No one really knew how to deal with him, how to teach him, in what way to help him. There was a common wisdom that he should be left to his own devices, in essence, ignored. This approach is practically criminal. Luckily, we were, as I said, not without resources, for my wife was a peculiar individual with a thousand odd thoughts.

The first thing that a person at The Shape School is taught is patience. In order to affect another person you perform some action. Then, you must be patient enough to wait for its effect. As you learn the signs of these effects, it may come to pass that you do not need to wait as long, but as my wife often said—it can happen that you say or do a thing, and the effect is felt years later, perhaps in a reiteration of the scene within a dream, who can say? Our actions echo—to be human is to tremble!

In any case, my wife was very patient and she would try a thing with our son, and then wait to see what came of it, and try another thing and wait to see what came of it, always persistently repeating the things, and giving enthusiastic reinforcement. There was no expectation that anything in particular would happen. The main thing was for him to feel that we were all together taking part in a joined project—the project of our life. To be a part of such a thing, he wanted nothing more than that. Indeed, it is what most of us want, isn't it? Why should he be any different?

She said to me, often, in the year before her death—it is a pity that she did not have her career as a clown after raising our son, for she felt that her powers of empathy and apprehension were increased a thousandfold by the experience. I can say truly that for me it was the same—I was a better doctor for having had my son, for it left me with a basic stance—that I should not expect anything in particular from anyone, nor should I underestimate anyone, a humility vested not so much in an appraisal of myself, as in a lack of confidence in valuation and prediction. This was the stance, as you know, that led me to the work of the census.

Somehow, the ongoing project I spoke of, the project of our life, that my wife, son and I were embarked on, had failed in the figure of my wife's corpse, and so we had no choice, my son and I, but to undertake some severe action, a reappraisal of sorts. For us that was the census, and so we began, and set out north passing through ring after ring, B and C and D and so forth. E and F and G.

Could it have been something else? Could that reappraisal have somehow appeared in an absolutely contrary form—perhaps an ocean voyage, my son and I on a ship as passengers, eating supper amidst white gloved waiters? That was not the spirit with which we lived our life—so at least that eventuality would not have appeared, but some other? It is hard to say. I know that my wife's desire to tour the country in the company of my son, myself, somehow hardened in my memory into an irresistible command that was stated by her death. And a simple tour, a tour with no purpose would be—how does one say it, it would be impossible or difficult to make any choices on such a tour. The census could somehow stand in for my wife, where before it would have been she, my son, myself, there now was another trifecta, myself, my son, the census. Held together by a common purpose, we did not need to wonder, and could simply feel.

When we crossed the river and came to J, we were speaking of the nice things that we would have. Like everyone else, when the day crawls on, we begin to speak of what we will have for dinner. I was going to have some kind of soup, a vegetable soup and maybe a grilled cheese sandwich—something nearly any roadside diner provides. My son had his heart set on a hamburger and after that perhaps some pie.

But there was no one in J anymore. The road through it was in good shape, as was the bridge over which we had come, but J was just a long line of shuttered businesses, collapsed roofs, concrete cracked with the festive and brutal hands of plants, the fingers of young trees.

We will have to keep on, I said. Our best plan is to open the peanuts and keep driving. As we drove, I kept picturing the diner we would come to, and the steam rising up from the soup that I would then get to eat.

I don't think that my wife was disappointed by my son. I don't think that she blamed herself, or blamed me. Her understanding of things was richer than that. But I do know that she sometimes wished we could have done more. There were things she had hoped to do, and now it is clear, now that she is dead: we simply did not do those things and won't. I suppose this is true of children in general, of any children, but it seems especially true of a child who must be cared for permanently. I never apologized to her for him, and she likewise never said anything to me about it. If such a feeling of unhappiness existed, it would only have been in the abstract, for the particular were: we felt lucky to have had him, and lucky to become the ones who were continually with him, caring for him. I have read some books of philosophy in which the freedom of burdens is explained, that somehow we are all seeking some appropriate burden. Until we find it, we are horribly shackled, can in fact scarcely live.

The people in the next town, which we came to early in the morning, told us, about J, that there had been a mine collapse, and the only local business that mattered had gone down. Everything else went too, and people fled. One old man still lives there. Perhaps you saw him?

The industry in K, which was not one town, but a set of them—three or four along a river, with fields on both sides—was farming.

The thing about farming, a man told me, as I marked him, is: *everything goes wrong*. Being a farmer is becoming used to every last thing going wrong. No one but farmers understand fairness.

What is there to understand? I asked.

That there isn't any.

The man's wife coughed and gave me a mug of coffee.

Miners think that they can just pull precious things out of the ground and get rich quick. But, what happens when the mine collapses?

I said that I thought mining was hard work too.

Oh it's hard work—it is hard work. But are you putting in the work? Are you? Are you waiting to see the fruits of it?

I didn't really understand his point, so I tried the coffee, which was terrible, and I praised it, and thanked them. I concluded my census business with the man, and then his wife and I attended to it in the back of the house, by a window overlooking the fields of their farm. She sat next to me on a bench, and I immediately felt her femininity. There is being a man, there is being a woman, being a boy, being a girl, etcetera. No woman is any more a woman than any other, obviously—everyone should have the freedom to be how they like, and to create it from nothing in fact. But there are some who are deeply conversant with what it has meant culturally to be a woman—and how that should appear, and they can sometimes surround themselves with a specific kind of forceful femininity. It doesn't even matter if they are young or old. This is something else I'm speaking of. I suppose I have even met a man who had it—that femininity. This woman and I, we sat on the bench, and I could close my eyes and draw her. That's part of it.

She told me a story about herself long ago. For me, this was the kernel that I required of her, and I needed no more as a census taker.

»

She said, when I met my husband, I was married to someone else. He, my first husband, was a foreman in the chemical plant in P. You will go there eventually, I guess, if you keep north on this road. We had a very large house, and two daughters. I was the prettiest girl in town and people were always telling me how lucky I was. You are so lucky, they would say. Two daughters who look just like you. But both my daughters died. There was some contaminant that my husband brought home on his clothes, and somehow it got to them. They were three and five at the time. I remember how small their bodies were. I couldn't understand anything that was told to me. All I could do was to leave him and to pretend it hadn't happened. I got on the bus with a small bag. I came here to this town. I married my second husband, continued the work I know how to do. We raised another girl, a daughter. She arrived the year after.

I named her after them, her first name is the name of my oldest daughter, her middle name the name of my second oldest daughter, her full name, the name then of all three, for I kept my name. She is gone now, too—went away to school and never returned, which is something I understand. You can't ever ask anyone to stay, can you? But this other thing I wonder about. What is the comfort in giving her their names, in using those names again? Why do we try to honor things by pretending they are anything like other things? Does it make any sense?

I said it didn't make sense—but that I understood, I felt I understood why she would do it. I asked what her husband thought about it all.

He doesn't know about it. I never told him.

She said she somehow knew eventually someone would come to whom she could speak about it, and until that time, she had been in no hurry. There is always enough to do, so she said.

The fields we looked out on were barren, entirely flat, for it was winter now and the sky held clouds from rim to rim. A bird at the far tree line disturbed the scene, which otherwise was as still as water. Every place you go to—when you are there you feel it is so far from anywhere else, in certain moods. In other moods I feel I can just rise up, almost out of my body and be anywhere else, or everywhere else. Do you know, have you felt that simultaneity?

The house was decorated all over with small cheerful gestures of color and texture. It seemed Swedish to me. I looked out the window again. A thin column of light was falling from a cloud—just like in a painting, and the field around it was shadowed and palled. Then the column spread and disappeared and then suddenly grew and the field was all light, everything in focus. Then the clouds came again.

The woman looked like someone I used to know, a patient of mine who fell from a window. I had fixed her leg and arm and in return she would sometimes bring us a basket of this or that. My wife liked her, though I did not. She would always ask me, why don't you like her? And I would invent reasons. I would say, she keeps too many dogs, she can't possibly know them all, or she wears a raincoat when it's sunny. This was the way my wife and I spoke to each other.

But I was there in the room not with the woman I disliked but with this farm woman who I did not know and could not—because I myself was no part of the interaction. I was there on the business of the census, beyond like or dislike.

Do you have any other questions for me? she asked.

It had been so many years, I said. Had she been back to P? Had she ever seen her first husband again, the foreman?

I would think he must have killed himself. He must have, he must have killed himself.

She said it with an accent on the word killed, but I couldn't tell what the accent was.

What do you think? she asked me. What would you have done in that circumstance? Wouldn't you have just killed yourself?

We went back in the other room where my son was playing checkers with the farmer. My son had three kings and was very happy with himself. The game had been a great success. The farmer had only one king and things were not looking good.

I took a picture of the two of them hunched over the board. My son still had his coat on, and the farmer's sleeves were rolled up.

The farmer was at that moment, the moment I took the picture, asking if they could agree to a draw. In reply, my son, never one to be hurried, especially not at his gladdest moments, moved one of his three kings, I doubt it even mattered which, and smiled down at the board where the teeth of the torn cobs spread like drawn suns.

The country is larger than anyone thinks it is. It contains more—contains so much that any survey will inevitably be made in error. Some think that the answer is to fly over in planes and photograph from above, so that nothing will be missed. The trouble is, things aren't the same from far above. I had often seen photographs and heard stories of the country north of the capital. I had heard of others who had made a travel similar to our own, and gone the road to Z. But I had heard very little about the area north of L.

As my son and I drove down the long slope putting K well behind us, I could see through the fogged glass of the window a long valley presented ahead and on either side. The remainder of our trip would be made in a sort of industrial hell interspersed with bands of what might be called wilderness, but what were, in essence, abandoned tracts, towns not thought worth exploiting, and the lands around them.

My condition pressed upon me as we went, and I felt again that we should stop, perhaps that we should even stop for some days, but the first motel we came to was filthy, and though we bought a room, my son would not enter it, and we ended sleeping in the car.

Will you please go in? Please?

He would not go in, not for anything.

The motel was the Leapley Motor Inn, and I confess that I did not want to sleep in the room either.

The next morning, we went to an apartment complex and knocked on the first door we came to.

My son and I had argued about whether people would be different here. Or rather, we both agreed they would be, but he thought they would be nothing like the ones before. I disagreed.

The first door was answered by a man of about fifty with a yellowish face and a moustache.

»

The census, huh. All right. Come in.

This man was a detective in the police force of L. He had served in that department for three decades, and in that time had seen almost anything that can happen to a person happen to a person, whether for good or ill.

His wife, a much younger woman, practically a girl, he told us, was out just then, but his son, age nine, was there. They sat next to each other on the couch and we sat across from them. Sometimes one would talk, sometimes the other.

At first the boy was confused about what we were after, which is understandable—since we weren't exactly after anything. However, the father, being an officer of the law, understood the census very well, and so he explained to the son what it was that we were supposed to be doing there. That meant that although in coming there we had a different purpose, our own purpose (as I have mentioned, in some ways estranged from the typical census activity), we were forced by circumstance to, in this case at least, readopt the general behavior of the census taker as it is typically known.

The son was holding a military style doll which was garbed in thick white cloth for some sort of winter campaign. The doll had a rifle in its hand that was also wrapped the same way.

Will you include Henry in the census? the boy asked.

His father told him that the question was an absurdity. Henry was a doll. He would not be included in the census.

I said, on the other hand, there is no real reason to avoid Henry. There would be so many mistakes in the manner that the census was conducted overall that to add Henry to the data would not cause too much harm. I pointed out also that potentially Henry, as the construction of a person in the culture at large, was likely to represent some consensus point, and should therefore not actually contradict any of the other data.

The father, as a veteran policeman, was quite conversant with the point of view that we should let sleeping dogs lie and conduct momentary affairs to best fit the situation.

All right then, Henry, he said. What do you think?

The boy mentioned that Henry would like to be introduced first.

The detective explained to us that his son had wanted the winter sniper soldier toy for the last six months, but that whenever they would go to the store, there would be no winter sniper soldier toys because they had all already been purchased. The toy store did not permit orders to be put in; you simply had to get there at the right time. Many of the boy's friends had the soldier toys, and several had the winter sniper soldier toy. Those who had it insisted it was by far the best one. The others were essentially placed around the house for the winter sniper soldier toy to notice and kill. Any other narrative was in dispute. By virtue of this schema, the soldier toys that the son owned were rendered useless for play, and in fact he became disconsolate and spent long hours staring into space.

Finally, about a week before our arrival, the detective had been called to a crime scene. A woman had committed suicide and taken her two children with her. The husband was at large, and was a suspect in a different case, one the detective was working on. While the detective was walking around the house examining things, his eye lit on what was to him a familiar and almost hated sight: lying prone beneath the bed of one of the dead children, the winter sniper soldier toy, rifle and all.

That's when I met Henry, he said. Henry needed a home. You can't just go around sniping all the time. At some point you need a home.

I began to have dizzy spells as we drove on, and occasionally I would be forced to stop the car for hours at a time. I often would have trouble breathing.

It seemed to me, as we made our visits, as we obtained the records we needed, that I was traveling not just into L and on to M and N, but that I was traveling into my own past, because as I grew fainter, I felt that I had begun to recognize the people that we came across, and when they told their stories to me, I felt I knew some of them already.

I kept having nightmares. In the nightmares, I was in the census office, and the census chief was telling me that I had filled out all the forms incorrectly, that every last thing I had sent in was going to be destroyed. He showed me what that destruction would look like. He led me to a room and threw open the door. At the far side, there was a sort of fire pit, and all the papers I had obtained were piled there. On the papers were huddled the tiny living shapes of the people I had met, and the whole thing had been set on fire—it was burning. That was one. In another I was cutting people's hair. For some reason, I was in the census office and cutting the hair of the employees, and I heard them talking about someone, and the person they were talking about was me. They said horrible things about me, and about my son, and they said there was something in wait for us, an awful end, an end that we ourselves should have expected. The humor of this was almost too much for them, and I had to keep asking them to stop moving so I could cut their hair, something they wouldn't do, they were enjoying their laughter too much. They kept thinking of new jokes to say about this census taker and his son—this absolutely stupid pair. Meanwhile, the line of people waiting to have their hair cut grew longer and longer.

In another, the bureau chief sat me down and asked me to explain what it was I thought I was doing. He said to me, you were supposed to visit every house in every town. You don't leave a town until you have visited every house. Don't you understand?

When I tried to explain why I had not done that, my voice would only come out in a whisper. I would whisper and he would ask me to speak up, and when I couldn't, he would hit me with the butt of his hand, a brief slap such as you give a child or a dog.

Get up, he kept saying, and if I tried to stand up, he would push me back into the chair.

»

I kept waking up each morning in the car. I felt almost imprisoned by it, yet it was also the only place I could feel any comfort, or if not comfort at least not hesitancy.

We started keeping to the car more and more and so I would wake in the car, we would wake in the car and the windshield would be right there in front of me, opaque, like the cover on a coffin, and I would feel that surely, implacably, I was in a coffin, but then I would hear my son's breath beside me. I would hear him; sometimes, even he would wake, and reach out his hand to me and we would hold hands. Then I could breathe and breathe and the day would begin.

I felt that I must continue to Z. There was nothing for it but to continue to Z. And at the same time, as my condition worsened, I felt sure that I would not make it to Z. What then? When there is nothing to do, you do what little there is—what little is left.

My wife wrote me letters when we first met. We lived in the same place—not together yet, obviously, but in the same city, and we would meet every day, or nearly every day, but still she would write me letters.

I just feel, she would say, that there are things I would never say to you—things you need to know.

Also, she thought the person she was in her letters was someone she herself did not know until the letter was written, and then it was like she was meeting herself.

She said that when she was at The Shape School, she lived nearby, with a young couple who had consented to take in three student boarders. The three were my wife, another girl named Gretchen, who was about seventeen, the same age as my wife, and a younger girl. The younger girl was totally uninteresting. Do you remember one of the vases at your aunt's house? Did you have an aunt? Did she have vases? Did you see those vases? This girl was like such a vase, impossible to notice, and instantaneously forgotten, not to be told apart from any other vase.

My wife said the couple was young and very successful. The house was quite large, with beautiful marble countertops, rooms leading on to rooms, two or three kitchens, verandas, porches. The man was an attorney, his spouse a chemist. Because the woman was a chemist, she spent long hours in the laboratory, and when she was there, the husband would be making love with Gretchen all over the house. He was very charismatic, and somehow he managed to obtain the understanding from the girls almost instantly that the whole thing was a lark, but should absolutely not be spoken of—it was something the girls had in common with him, this was what he communicated. Meanwhile, the wife would sit the three girls down and give them advice about the world, and how to handle themselves as women. She would touch Gretchen on the wrist and say, you have to think about things from every angle. Gretchen would laugh—she had a hoarse laugh like a donkey, and she would laugh. It was so funny to her—the woman talking about angles.

Still, my wife was just a girl then and loved going to The Shape School. She had found a place, as she put it, between wing beats. The bird sails on through the air. The teachers praised her constantly, but also pushed her, cursed her even. At The Shape School one of the instructors for the final year even used a quirt, a short whip, to bring the students to heel. He used the whip on her.

My wife relates that one day she showed up to class wearing just pants—nudity was common at The Shape School, and the instructor whipped her so hard that the whip cut her just below the collarbone. Why did she get whipped? She got whipped for not noticing what was happening. Her shirtlessness had nothing to do with it.

One of the rules at The Shape School was, when you enter a room you had best know immediately what is happening. Every last thing that is happening in the room, you must acquire, process and place. Acquire, process and place. Then you can know how to behave. You should even be able to shut your eyes and reconstruct the scene.

On that day, she was late and thinking about something else, so when she rushed into the classroom, she failed to notice that a dog was giving birth on the table. In coming into the rooms so rapidly, she alarmed the dog. This led to her correct punishment at the hands of her teacher.

I always liked her, though, she wrote to me in the letter detailing these events, I always liked her even when she whipped me. Her lessons were brutal. There was no way to leave the classroom unchanged.

In another one of her letters she speaks about her boyfriend Willy. He was not at The Shape School; he went to school in the nearby town. But he suspected her of constantly having sexual orgies at The Shape School, a thing that, to the best of my wife's knowledge, had never and would never happen at The Shape School. Still, the general lawlessness, physical contact, and irreverence of The Shape School led him to believe that such things went on, and he was always trying to catch her in a lie. In spite of that, he was a dear boy, so she said, and she would perhaps have married him, but for one thing. One day, we were talking and he said something to me. The thing that he said was so awful that I resolved never to speak to him. Much as I loved him, much as I wanted to spend the rest of my life with him, he said this one thing and it was too much. I knew instantly that I would never speak to him or see him again. I will tell you in the next letter what that thing was.

Well, of course I was curious as to what that thing was that Willy had said. I was also a little worried—I had only met this young woman recently, I liked her very much; I didn't want to say the wrong thing to her and receive the same treatment Willy had. But the days went by, I saw her each day, and the next letter failed to materialize. I became a little concerned. One day as we were walking in the city gardens, she turned to me:

You must be curious what Willy said to me.

I told her I was. I was very curious.

The truth is: I never knew anyone named Willy. We weren't allowed to have relationships at The Shape

School. Matter of fact, we had to sign a document saying we never would. The instructors of The Shape School believed that people are individuals and must remain so. I was never meant to know or love anyone any more than anyone else. Aren't you glad I am failing at that?

A long time ago I had an apartment over a bakery. The walls and floors were thin, and in the night I could hear the bakers arriving and going about their early ministrations. Rather than to say that it was a nuisance, I will here record—I dearly loved this noise, and in fact I have never slept so well as when I could wake occasionally and hear the comforting sounds of baking going on below. When the time came to get up, I would go to the window, a gigantic floor to ceiling window on one side of the, admittedly, shabby apartment, and I would throw it open and sit for a time on a little terrace there, looking down over the main street. It was an old part of the city and many of the people became familiar to me. They loved those streets, and I loved them too, and none of us liked going out of them into the city at large.

For many at that hour, their destination was the bakery, so in a sense, I would sit on the terrace and watch as the people of that quarter came to me and went away, where I sat on a sort of mast extruded from the forehead of the beast that was the bakery. I was so happy then, and I was happy because in that year an amazing thing happened: *I became certain that I would find someone I could love.* Before that, I had an equal certainty, an equal and opposite certainty, motivated by experience and rational thought, and this equal certainty told me, you who have never found anyone of real worth, you shall never find anyone of real worth, and the reason is this: people are islands and all communication is impossible. There is only fakery, mummery, and a dulling of the senses.

Yet one day I had a dream. It was the night before my surgical examinations, and I had a dream in which I was garbed in a silver fabric from head to toe. I was standing in a meadow and the sun and moon were close above my head, and as I said, I was garbed in a silvery fabric, and this fabric allowed me to feel for once an absolute happiness in my limbs and my features. I called out—but without need, just a cry, just a golden cry, and someone came to me out of the darkness. There were trees all about the meadow and in the trees, I could feel that there were thousands of people waiting, staring, holding their arms to themselves. From that group in thrall there came one—a girl—and her face was turned away so I could not see it, but she came closer and closer, and I called again and she came closer. I woke there in my room, and the noise of the baking was below, the sound of the bakers' talk. I crossed the room, my feet almost glowing against the warm floorboards, and when I threw open the window, I felt a thousand other windows, other doors opening. Somehow I knew I had stumbled upon some key, and that it would not be long before I met a person I could love.

I did not have long to wait. Perhaps a month, perhaps two months—then, I was standing on a corner, consulting some directions I had written on the back of my hand, and a girl bumped into me. I'm sorry, she said, I'm sorry to tell you this, but that guy over there, the one crossing the street. I think I saw him take your wallet.

I reached into my pocket. It was as she said: the wallet was gone. My eyes went to where the man had been a moment before, but he was no longer there. Then, I saw him, turning the corner, slightly further on. I began to chase him, but the girl ran after me, saying, wait, wait, wait, and wait again.

You have probably already guessed it, but she had taken the wallet. She gave it back to me and asked me where I was going so absent mindedly. I said sarcastically that I was about to speak to a congregation on the subject of kindness to strangers, and the general lack of it. Would she like to come along as an example?

She did not laugh.

But really, where were you going?

To a party—someone is giving a party. I don't know anyone there.

She smiled and twined her arm with mine.

In that case, she said, let us go together you and I. We'll pretend we are sister and brother, but also lovers. What do you think? We will be holding back our affection because we are in public, but there will be something there—something obvious to everyone. What do you think?

Now, at that time, I should mention, my wife to be was already a tremendous success. It happened that I did not know her, and, of course, she liked that. It was probably even necessary for me to not know her.

In any case, she lived in a very beautiful house outside of the city, and had a large barn there where her performances were planned. She was not going to move out of it on my account, so the only thing to do was for me to move out of my place. However, there was one problem with that. She had, by that time, grown to enjoy going to visit me there, and she liked especially looking up from the street and seeing my silhouette in the window of the little studio (there was almost nowhere you could go in the room where you could not be seen from outside).

This is an example of the way that she thought. Her solution to the problem—the problem being that I would no longer be in that apartment because I would be living elsewhere with her—was that she bought the apartment outright. She bought it, and then we would only rent it to people who resembled what I looked like at that time. A string of men all resembling me in height and silhouette.

So it was possible then, for many years, even down to the time of her death, to walk there in the old quarter and behold in the window my old self doing this or that, such things as I did when I lived there.

She was very thin, my wife, always very thin, and her face looked a little like a ferret. You would never trust her with anything, to look at her. She was on the small side, and wore loose clothing, although when she wanted to, she could certainly appear to be rather large, or even smaller. This was part of her art.

She had long fingers and a mole under her left eye that looked like a tear. Her irises were flat gray, like a sheet of rain, and she would often look through you when you talked. People would always be turning around to see what she was looking at.

She wasn't very strong, but she had done tremendous physical training for her work, and she was very fast—shockingly fast. I remember, she and my son were on a train, he was very young, maybe five, and somewhat frail, and a man started making fun of my son, so she didn't hesitate; she hit the man in the face and broke his nose. The police came, and there was going to be trouble, but the other people in the car wouldn't testify that anything had happened.

She found out the man's address, though, and we sent him a box of specially fabricated chocolates—a half dozen noses. This was her sense of humor. When we explained it to the chocolatier he didn't even charge us.

»

From the moment I met her, I immediately ceased to feel alone. I became, if anything, more secretive with others, because whatever I thought of to say, I could say it better, and have it heard better, saying it to her, than to anyone else.

Sometimes she would try to convince me to be playful in my work, to leave a clamp or a forceps inside one of my patients with a note on it for the person who would eventually get it out—things like that. Of course, I never did any such thing.

I often wonder, though, what drew her to me in the first place. She said it was because my emotions are all slightly garbled. She saw me in the street and watched me—it was something she used to do all the time as training for her performances, to follow people and try to feel what they are thinking, try to copy what they are doing. She found that I was very hard to copy, not because I was bluff, but for some other reason, a reason I don't know.

drove sometimes for hours, and in such cases, I would stop only because my son would pull and pull at my arm. At other times, I would sit in the car, staring at the glass, almost incapable of making any forward motion. At such times, my son would wait patiently—his patience was a thing of legend—and he would sing, and soon the clouds would pass and we would continue. Many times I could actually not breathe and I felt that it was the end, but then a moment would come and go and a moment, and then I would be breathing.

There was a porch I remember we pulled up to, it was either in M or N, there was no yard, just cars parked all over the place, and we pulled up right next to the porch and went in.

A couple guys, mechanics, were lounging on the front steps. We spoke to them for a while, and then I marked them, and then we went on in. It was a men's boarding house, many single rooms with shared hall bathrooms. The place was run by a positively Rabelaisian fat man who stomped about with an almost ornamental broom, cursing everyone.

He sat us down in his own personal apartment, which, it turned out, was exactly the same as everyone else's. That meant we, my son and I, sat on the single pallet, and he sat on the single chair across from us, and I wrote down what he said, everything he said, as best I could.

He said, I was a soldier, of course, and a good one. I joined as a private, but ended a captain. That doesn't happen very often. As they say, only in wartime. These guys are always asking me how many people I've killed. How many people have you killed, how many people have you killed, he said, imitating the voices of his young charges. I always tell them—a hundred, two hundred, take your pick. A machine gunner never counts. Why?

He laughed, a great bellowing laugh.

Because he's too busy, he's too busy. First I was a machine gunner, then I was in charge of a whole bunch of trucks and tanks. I ran them the same way I run this lot. The same way.

He showed us a tattoo of a lion that he had on his arm. The tail wrapped around the bicep and went up almost to the neck where it was a fire hose being used by silhouettes of firemen to put out a fire that was raging actually on his neck. There was a house that was the house that we were in, and it was on his neck, and it was being put out by a fire hose which was in reality the tail of a lion. That's what he showed us when he showed us his tattoo. My son did not like it at all. He doesn't like tattoos. But I thought it was wondrous.

How did you come to live here? I asked him.

I've always lived here. This was my childhood home. My parents ran the boarding house, same as I do, although we lived in the basement then.

He showed us a picture of his father and mother, who essentially looked alike. They both looked exactly like him.

How much do you charge for a room? I asked him.

I take one-sixth of their pay—so that the boys can always afford it. That includes meals, by the way, so it's real fair. It's real fair.

Do you know how I find them? How I find this lot?

I said I didn't know.

He said they come to him. He's never had to go looking for a single tenant. Everytime they come to him, all the time, the rooms are full.

Do you want to see a list? He took out a list that was in a box on the table. You probably can't count it, just looking, but there are more than a hundred names there. That's the waiting list. Streng's Boarding House for Men Only. It's not a winning proposition—I don't make very much off it, but I feel, it's a kind of community, and I like to have them around.

There isn't time to show it to you, but if you went down to the cafeteria you'd see, more than sixty pictures on the wall, one per year, going back to my parents' time, all the boarders lined up, proprietor in the middle, that's my right.

He showed us a couple more things before we left, a carved horn he had brought back from abroad, a board with his medals on it.

I won't see you out, he said, I have to get back to this.

As I shut the door, I looked back through it and saw
he was sitting on the bed where we had been sitting,
and now, with a needle and thread, was mending
something, maybe a shirt. Our eyes met and the door
closed.

»

We went into the very next street where there was a
little cottage between two five-story apartment buildings. I knocked on the door. A woman in a bright blue
housecoat let us in. I can't hear anymore so you will
have to write down what you want to ask, she said.
I wrote down on a piece of paper, I AM A CENSUS
TAKER DOING THE CENSUS. Oh, the census, she
said. I like that.

I waited to see if she would say anything else, but she
went into the other room and came back with more
paper and a tray with a pot of coffee and some cheap
cookies, they must have been several years old. Here
you go, she said. I am ready.

She said that she had lived there her entire life. She
used to live in the house next door, her parents had
owned both, but that was demolished sixty years
before. Ever since then she had lived in the house in
which we sat. She had been a teacher—geography.
Did we know our geography? I said that I was a bit
unsteady with mine. She thought that was a shame
and said all people should know geography because it
is a good investment of time. It is information that will
as she put it stand you in good stead. Learning about
other things is often useless because these other
things they change so fast. You might learn about
them, sure you can, but then the next week no one
cares. The information is reduced to as she said trivi-
ally small proportion. Whereas with geography it is a
different time scale. You learn something and it will be
good for most of if not all your life.

Her husband had been a kind of technician—he could
fix televisions, ovens, radios, that sort of thing. The

whole back of the house, I won't take you there, but I could, was his workshop and it is still full of all his things. I know that I could get rid of them, I could have the whole house to put things in, but I don't have anything else to put there, you see, and anyway, it would break my heart to see his tools piled up on the curb.

She asked me why I was going around at my age. You don't look so well, she told me. I hate to say this to a grown man, but you don't look so well. Someone else should have said it to you already.

I said people had been telling me so, and I knew it myself. I was a doctor before I was a census taker.

This took her by surprise, and she didn't like it at all. Evidently, she had an entirely different code of behavior for how to be around doctors and people of that sort, and I had in some way forced my way in to the house as a census taker, when in fact, I was a doctor, etcetera.

Unfortunately, the incident could not recover from this epiphany, and we made our departure shortly after. I couldn't write out the proper thing to fix it—maybe I could have said the proper thing, but with her hearing problem and me having to write it out on a sheet of paper and show it to her, it wasn't possible, not for me. At the door, she regretted her hostility, and she pressed some cloth napkins on my son, monogrammed ivory napkins. You'll need these if you are traveling, she said, and hugged him.

When my wife was pregnant with my son, we had many talks about possible futures—things we would do, ways that things would go. She thought that she would perhaps go back to performing and traveling. Perhaps even the three of us would travel together. She imagined that her son or daughter might become a performer like her. Don't performers go about in families? she would say. All of this dreaming came to an absolute halt on the day of the birth when our son appeared. I don't mean to give the impression that we were unhappy, because we weren't, we weren't unhappy at all. It was just that a sheer wall had appeared confining us and our lives in certain ways that we could never have guessed at before. My wife said to me about it—I think that my whole life before was training for this. If that was so, it was a lucky thing, because our son certainly needed someone around who knew how to behave with him, and how to help him. And in our life, we saw many other families who were not as successful in handling the special demands of the situation.

There were children in the neighborhood, who, as he grew, would come to play with him, but they changed so quickly, grew so fast, they would outgrow him in a year or so, and he would be alone again. In this way we became his main companions and playfellows. My wife did not return to the stage, there just wasn't time for it, and, in truth, I think having our son made her like people less in general, I know it made me like them less.

Liking them less, she no longer wanted to perform for them. How could it be, we asked ourselves again and again—that they are all so cruel to him? How can this enormous conspiracy exist—where everyone has agreed ahead of time that it is completely all right to be hurtful to these harmless people who hurt no one?

The situation in some ways tinges everything with the sadness of these inevitable encounters. People's ignorance was so sharp then, it is still sharp now, and many of them cannot perform so much as a basic interaction without saying something base and awful, or laughing or outright turning away.

It is true, though, that there is another side, which is that it made it easier to find the people who are worthwhile, as they were and are in no way troubled by him, and would enter into an immediate camaraderie. Such a person is difficult to guess at—I would not always have known them from their appearance, for people with innate gentleness and sensitivity are often compelled to hide or disguise it.

In any case, this is how we ended up making our friends—by pushing away people we thought brutal, and gathering to ourselves those we thought kind and subtle.

It was hard though for me, as a doctor, when a patient of mine would say something thoughtless and awful, and then I would be in a position thereafter to affect that person's life. So many times I wanted to leave the patient with a little punishment, a twinge in the knee, a slight limp, a pronounced scar. But it is not a thing I ever did.

»

We came into a house where the door was open. Is anyone here? A man was sitting on a stool in the kitchen, with his shirt off. He was about my age. He engaged us in conversation and when he learned what we were after, he began to tell us all kinds of things. He said that he was the representative for his union, the boilermaker's union, and that he was currently conducting extremely, as he put it, clandestine, negotiations regarding salary and benefits. The negotiations were going on nearby and he had just run out to take a breather. If we thought it strange that he was not wearing a suit, well, that was part of the situation. He didn't want anyone to know exactly what was going on.

His wife came into the room. What are you doing here? He explained to her what we were doing there. She addressed us again, what are you doing here? I explained what he had explained: that we were there on the business of the census, and simply asking questions, recording answers, and so forth. She nodded, seemingly surprised that my answer was in accord with his.

This way, she said.

And when he got up to follow, she said, severely,

Not you. You stay put. You stay right there.

We went into the next room, which was a parlor with a big television set facing a dirty couch. It was lined with bookshelves and on the bookshelves were those books that are actually the spines of books taped together to look as if the person has all the classics.

I don't know what he just told you, but he is very ill. My husband is sick. He won't take his medication today, and it would be better for all of us if you would just leave. I can't believe you came in here in the first place. What a piece of shit you are. You've gotten him worked up, and it will take me at least an hour to get him back to where he was.

I stood up. My son held my hand.

Please excuse us.

The woman's face was furious. Her body was agitated.

She saw us to the door. The man was behind her. He had stood up and he was shouting about something. His voice was really thin in places, like it had been worn out. She pushed us through and shut the door. As we went down the steps, the door opened again and she stuck her head out.

Don't come back!

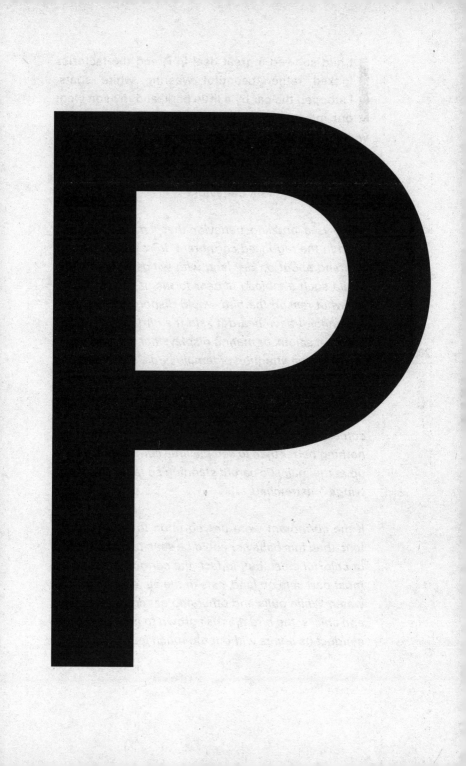

It had snowed a great deal in P, and the factories looked rather beautiful wearing white coats. I stopped the car by a little park, and my son went out into the snow and adventured there. Meanwhile, I turned the heat on and read from Mutter. I enjoy reading her books aloud, and so I sat reading aloud from With Wings Outstretched, her monograph on cormorant behavior.

There is a puzzling behavior that I myself first noticed in the rag-faced cormorant. It is: the propensity to stand about on dry land with wings outstretched. While such a tableau is dear to me, it is hard to say for what reason the bird would disport itself in such a manner. I have heard it said the bird is performing a kind of salute, or mating display, that the purpose is to attract the attention of female birds. But males and females both perform this gesture, and furthermore, have been observed doing it when alone. It is also the case that cormorants with young, which, as a rule, come once in the year, will perform this gesture. I like nothing better than to see the little cormorants gazing up at the majestic parent standing so far above them, wings outstretched.

If the cormorant were preyed upon to any great extent, then this behavior could be seen to be some sort of colorful crest, but, in fact, the cormorant is for the most part safe on land, safe in the air, and safe in the water. While gulls and others do eat cormorant eggs and chicks, the bird that has grown to adulthood may conduct its affairs without too much fear.

I believe that the cormorant is a sort of laundress, and that the gesture is done merely to dry the wings. The bird likes, as we all do, to have its clothing dry, and so it stands and lets the wind do its work. There are those who think otherwise, and I will let them.

The door opened and my son was back in the car, covered in snow. I wrapped him in a horseblanket and we continued through the wintry landscape towards the gigantic electric sign of a restaurant, some blocks distant.

»

The town is named after a city in Spain, so the waitress told me, in Spain or in Portugal, one of the two. I apologized for tracking snow into the restaurant and her response was: I don't have to clean it up. He cleans it up, so I don't care.

She pointed to a man who stood at the back of the restaurant holding a mop loosely in one hand while reading a magazine with the other.

What is it you want?

She set us up with a large meal. We must have ordered most of what was on the menu, including some sort of spiced wine, which I drank happily.

When she came back she asked why we were there. No one willingly comes to P, she said. It must be for work. It is for work, I told her. I'm a census taker. I knew you were, I just knew it, she said, clapping her hands together.

How did you know?

Well, I saw that.

Sticking out of the corner of my bag was the tattooing apparatus.

Tattoo artists don't really carry their gear around. At least, it's not common. Anyway, you hardly ever see a tattoo artist over fifty. I just put two and two together: who else tattoos people?

She leaned in and unbuttoned her dress:

I don't have the mark yet from this one, but I'm ready. I love, I just love to be tattooed. She showed me some of her tattoos. You ever met anyone like that?

I said well let me finish the meal, and then we'll go through the whole rigmarole.

She thought that was okay, but then she kept coming back. I should explain that the restaurant was empty. The cooks were playing cards in the back with a radio going.

It's five now. Five o'clock. The workers don't start coming in until seven she said, when the chemical factories close. It'll be a parade.

She said she was an actress when she was young. When I was young, I was an actress, she told me, although she could have been no more than twenty-five as she stood there. I had a few roles, a few big roles. Then I got into trouble. I like to gamble. Do you like to gamble?

I said I did like to gamble, but I almost never did.

That's right, she said. You have to cut off the arm as soon as you can tell it's poisoned.

I got into trouble, I owed too much—had to leave. So I came here a few years back and guess where I am? I'm still here.

I said that she could go somewhere else if she wanted to.

She said, I bet you want to know what it was—what I bet on, don't you? It was the horses. I inherited a house from my parents, both dead now, and I mortgaged it and bet the full amount on a tip.

I said it must have been a good tip.

She said she was mathematically inclined, always mathematically inclined as a child, and she worked it out—she would only have to win this one bet, on a horse, which, mind you, should have been the favorite, but was not, and then she would never have to do another thing, not even one thing in her whole life. Now she had to do all kinds of things she didn't want to do. But did she regret it? No, she did not regret it. She had read a book once, one of her aunts gave it to her, it said, have no regrets, never have any. So she never did. She took it literally, she explained—she, as a girl, thought that it meant, don't let yourself regret things, rather than, go out and do the thing that you long to do, so you don't regret not having done it. She took it the other way, and in fact, to her mind, the other way is the way to take it. It's the better principle, on the whole. Anytime you think you are about to feel regret, just think about something else. There are plenty of things to think about, aren't there?

I don't drink, she said. I don't drink and I don't smoke. I stay fit, and I have read every book in the library next to the apartment building I live in, two streets down from here, some of them twice. I sleep five hours a night, I don't need any more than that, and the rest of the time I come up with plans, but I haven't done any of them yet. I have nothing to do with the dead-end men who come into this terrible restaurant. I'm just waiting for something to happen—if that horse was one side of the coin, I know there's another side, and I know it will come.

She brought us flan for dessert, on the house. I never eat it, she said, but I like to see people eat it. Flan brings so much happiness. Why is that? Do you even know how to make it? Do you know what it's made of?

The diner seats were heavily cushioned, and when I went to stand I almost fell.

It's all right, I said. I'm all right.

You are on your last legs, the waitress told me, laughing. Let me help you to the car.

We passed out through the hulking plants of P and beyond it there were marshes frozen over with winter. The road ran flat through the marshes, and soon there was nothing, no buildings, no lights, just reflectors on either side of the road, which luckily, was kept plowed.

After an hour or so of the road running straight, we came out of the marsh, and there was a crossroad with a gas station and a motor inn, and more factories rising out of a sort of standing fog. I asked my son if we should stop. I had to wake him up to do it.

Want to stop? I asked.

He sat up straight and looked out the window at the motor inn. Then he shook his head and slumped back into the blankets.

All right, all right then. I filled the car up with gas at the station, spoke to the attendant, who was a naturally angry man, and we went on.

At one of the schools that my son went to there was a teacher, a very wonderful man named Pearson. He had worked with children for many years, and had a very comforting presence. Children would speak to him who would speak to no one. We weren't sure why, but he had a very miraculous track record. The problem was that our son didn't want to be left there at the school. He didn't like the idea. When one of the teachers thought of trying Mr. Pearson, we agreed, despite the fact that he was a teacher for higher grades. I think, however, he also taught some experimental education classes. He was a very tall and severe looking man with a hook nose. Apparently he always wore a vest.

We entered the room and were introduced, and we introduced Mr. Pearson to our son. They stood there looking at each other, and Pearson said, Do you know, I sometimes like to draw or say a thing before I do it. It makes me feel good, and it helps me to know about how it might go, and what I might like or might not like about it. Do you want to try it? They went over to a little table that was there and on a big sheet of construction paper, Pearson wrote, we will be friends and today we'll go around the school together and see what is here. I will always ask before we do things if you are ready to do them and if you're not, we won't. If you're not ready we'll just keep doing what we were doing, or go back to something we were doing before. At the end of the day, you'll go home and you'll have lots of things to tell your parents.

Then Pearson explained what he had written down, going over it several times. My son nodded as if he understood from the very first. He took the pencil and made many lines there on the paper, as I told you he liked to do. Then he told Pearson about what he had written, though I could not hear what he said, and that was that. The two of them went out of the room and off down the hallway, and my wife and I had to find our own way out.

My most crucial memories I tread upon and I have tread upon some of them so often that when I am remembering them, I am inhabiting the space of my enjoyment—of my enjoyment of those crucial memories—at each and every moment that I sought them out before. Then I am many versions of myself, and all together we are aching with fondness over some minute thing, some small thing I noticed, years before, perhaps in passing, a thought that has returned to me again and again and again, sometimes growing, sometimes diminishing.

One such:

I would come back to the house often late at night from surgery, and I could see through the window my wife and son sitting at the kitchen table. The house was built in a sort of L shape with a barn on the far side and a high fence creating a hollow yard within which the car would sit. I usually walked from work, however, so I would come up to the outside of the atrium, where the kitchen window was placed, and through it I would see them.

That was their preferred place, the kitchen; I believe it is a preferred place for many of us, is it not?

And what would they do at the kitchen table? My son would often draw. My wife would work on a book she was writing, a book she had almost completed at the time of her death. It was called, *A Fool is a Mirror,* and was a sort of course that one could put oneself through—a course on clowning (although as I have mentioned, her clowning was not very similar to what is generally thought of as clowning).

As the newspaper put it, years ago, *If she is a clown, she is a very strange clown. She is one of those performers who gives a sense that there is no performance, it is just life and we happen to see it.*

I would stand there beneath that window for minutes at a time, just watching them. He would show her what he had done or she would show him some diagram from her book, or she would read aloud some part, and he would listen. There is a school of thought that says you should give people only what they can visibly understand. We never did that with him, but always spoke to him as if he was just like anyone else. I believe this made it possible for him to deal with regular people out in the world. It also makes clear a point, which is—I never knew which part of what I say he would receive. Sometimes I think the three of us could even have gotten along without any spoken language at all.

He would sometimes become frustrated, very frustrated, because we would set goals for him, and it would happen that we, who knew nothing about what would turn out to be possible or impossible, had helped him to set a goal that was too much. This was enormously depressing for him. On the other hand, if we set goals that were too easy, then he would lose interest, or what's worse, struggle with those out of some expectation that this easier thing was as hard as some other hard thing we had recently shown to him. There had to be a happy balance, though, and we learned it in time. Mostly it was a matter of mood— keeping a strong mood of joyfulness and gratefulness, and trying not, in our attitudes or speech, to lay the world out in hierarchies.

I remember the day he learned to do a particular sword move. He had a wooden sword, and he liked to swing it around out by a tree near the barn. He would go out there early in the afternoon and then it would be dusk and he would still be playing away, fighting invisible duels. In this case, he wanted to do a move that involved turning around in a circle and ending with a sort of horizontal slashing blow. You have probably seen it done once or twice. However that may be, the spinning around was very difficult for him. His legs would end up in the wrong place, and he would even become angry. So my wife practiced it with him and practiced it with him, the turning, going very slowly, again and again, very slowly, until finally, one day, he managed it. Of course, even then it wasn't exactly the spinning blow that a swordsman would use. He still took quite a bit of time in the turning around—however it was enough. I heard him calling to me all the way from the downstairs of the house, and I heard him on the stairs, and then in the hall by my study door. A part of me is, I think, still there behind that door, full of joy, listening to his approach.

often think of my son's experiences, and I compare them to my own—to the life that I have been lucky enough to live.

There was a man I knew—he used to wear a yellow suit, which is a pretty rare suit. To wear a suit like that you have to be certain of a lot of things. He frequented a twenty-four-hour chess cafe, one I went to compulsively when I was in medical school. I don't remember what his profession had been—perhaps he never said—but he knew an awful lot about ornithology, and it was he who got me on to Mutter. We would have wild games—any opening named after an animal, he knew it. His favorite was probably the Orang-Utan, a versatile beginning in coffeehouse chess as it leaves the second player confused and intimidated, if it is at all possible to intimidate him/her. But he loved to play the Hippo, the Dragon, the Polar Bear. Once he started c4 and I ran the game into the Hedgehog, one of my own personal favorites: he greeted my moves with applause and then proceeded to dequill me. We spent a lot of time together, perhaps those hours between 1am and 4am are especially long, most particularly for old bachelors, which he certainly was. In any case, he used to say to me: read widely because almost nothing has been everywhere applied. What does this mean? I took it to mean—insights are often made locally and used locally, but that a person with a wide range of interests will find the mirror of one thing in another and voila—there you have it—suddenly, the insight from one field appears perfectly suited to another. Or perhaps there are some changes to be made, but nonetheless . . .

I bring it up because the feel of that middle-of-the-night world is one I had not felt before, and one I have not found since. It is a thing confined in my heart to a small elliptical space, and beyond it there is nothing, no bridge to the rest. Or if there is a bridge, it is simply my shared love of the cormorant, or more precisely, of Mutter's cormorants, of what she felt about cormorants.

I am sad for my son that he has never gotten to go out on his own and find a world like that, a place where your small gestures of courtesy can be received with a slight but sure gravity. The kindnesses and at the same time the absolutely unforgiveable breaches made by old men playing chess: they are too many, far too many to name! They are all trivial, every last one, but together, they make a cosmos, and it was one I adored. I don't even remember the final visit that I made to that coffee house. My life became very busy, I had little time for such things. I got to know a series of women who would not let me roam about in the night, culminating in the end in my wife, a woman who certainly would have let me roam about in the night, but, in the company of whom, I was absolutely content, and so she, as much as the others, brought my nighttime chess playing to a close.

When the game became really intense, when it was close, and he would perhaps be defeated, this man in the yellow suit had a thing that he would say to me.

He would pause and look over the board, and then look up at me with an extremely serious look. He would wait for me to meet his gaze and he would say, the same way everytime:

In my city, they have a tradition—there must be a place at the table for the bride's father. Are you the bride's father?

I would say, I am not the bride's father.

Then he would say, are you the bride?

I would say, I am not the bride.

What then are you doing at the table?

At which point he would have figured a way out, and he would slam down one of his pieces in triumph and look up at me with a little smirk.

What then are you doing at the table?

My wife had a show that she performed once—it was a show in which only two dozen tickets were sold. These two dozen people came to the theater and sat in their seats. The show was to be an hour long. It was called, PRESENCE.

She sat on a chair at the front of the stage, simply dressed, with a trumpet on the ground next to her, and didn't say or do much of anything. She just watched the audience intently. The lights were on, so she could see them just as well as they could see her, and if they tried to talk, one of the ushers would quiet them down. Eventually, people left, in ones and twos until the theater was empty.

Then, within the next month, she showed up inside of all their houses, blowing this tremendously loud horn, and frightening many of them in the night.

She would hand them a letter and the letter said, *It is your life, your presence is required. You can't say where a thing will happen.*

Some people said at the time that she was lucky not to have been shot. The truth was a little different than that, however.

To my mind, if she had been shot, if she had been killed while performing this elaborate piece of buffoonery, well, I am certain she would have seen it as complete, as one of the ways of the matter ending.

»

In my office, which was in a little modern building—actually modern, not the farce that stands in for modern buildings these days—the patients waited beside a large glass window that looked onto a half acre of pines. The secretaries sat opposite, and through a door there was an entry to the rooms where I and my partner would meet our patients, who usually had been sent to us via physicians.

The building was polished concrete on the outside, with long vertical slits in it to let in the light. When it rained, you would find the falling of the rain in unusual places, and that was because the windows of the building, and the skylights were in unusual places. Alternately, at midday when the sky was clear, there were other effects: The bathroom that the doctors and secretaries used had a chisel shaped skylight that in the middle of the day brought a beam of light down, a beam of light that reminded me of pictures, photographs of light falling in cells in the panopticon. The light was supposed, as I recall, to be redemptive. I found this very funny, and pointed it to out to the secretaries, to all the various secretaries through the years. Some found it funny, some did not.

It happened occasionally that when I went to the office I would bring my son, and he always got along very well with the secretaries, and the nurses, especially when he was still a child. They would neglect their duties in order to play with him, and of course I always looked the other way. I remember standing in one of the narrow hallways looking out through a slit no more than six inches across, and seeing outside, where the pine trees congregated, one of the nurses in a crisp uniform, the fabric bent like a coat of feathers, kneeling on the pine needles, her childish face flushed and joyed with my son leaping and leaping in front of her, he too flushed and joyed, and the sensation in my body of all the years we would have together, and all the people he would get to meet and be.

My wife and I always spoke of making a trip together to show our son the country, but it never came. For one reason or another, it never came, and so I felt when my wife passed, when the idea rose in me about the census, I felt finally it was the time to take out the Stafford, to drive the roads north. In her death, I felt a sure beginning of my own end—I felt I could certainly not last much longer, and so, as life is vested in variety, so we, my son, myself, we had to prolong what life we had by seeing every last thing we could put our eyes upon.

Never mind the dangers, never mind the worries, or the troubles of the road. I felt sure all problems would solve themselves.

»

I stopped the car at the sign for the road leading up into S. I had decided to explain to my son what was happening.

I told him that I was having symptoms that pointed to a serious problem with my heart. Did he remember what the heart does?

We talked about what the heart does. I said that I needed mine if I was going to live, but that it looked like the heart was not going to work anymore.

I explained that we were very far from home, and from anyone that we knew, but that in Z there was a train and that he could perhaps take that train back to the place where we lived, and I could write ahead and there would be someone to meet him.

He said that sounded good to him, that he would enjoy it if we wouldn't drive in the car anymore. The two of us could go on the train. He wouldn't mind that.

I said that the thing was, it wouldn't be me going on the train with him, it would be just him. He would be on the train by himself.

But where would I be?

I said that I would not be anymore—it would have been the end for me. I pointed out that we had talked about death before, and how it is very natural, it is not something to be afraid of.

He thought that was fine, but he would prefer if we went on the train together. He could look forward to that.

I said that the plan had changed and now we were going to drive straight through to Z.

He liked that idea. He asked if we would have to stop at any more houses. I said we would not stop at any more. We were finished with that.

I went to the back of the car and started packing his things up, so they could fit together into a single bag. When he saw me doing this, he started packing my things into one of the other bags. I told him it was no use. I could not go on the train.

I continued putting his things in his rucksack, and he tried to stop me, he grabbed my arm, and when I wouldn't let him, he began to cry. I told him to sit in the front and wait. Instead he sat on the ground, right there, with his back to me.

When we got into S, I stopped at the post office and mailed a letter and we continued, and all through S and T he wouldn't speak to me at all.

In U, I had another episode and I lay flat on the ground until somebody came to help me and we were stuck there overnight. I got some pills at a pharmacy, and I was okay, or as well as was possible.

When the sun rose, and we began the drive, I saw that the factories had ended, the great procession of factories had ended, we had reached the cessation of the industrial corridor, that perhaps from here on in we would be driving through forest.

I felt giddy, uplifted.

I began to sing a song about a tree and my son joined in, we sang that song and other songs, and the road fell away beneath us. Now and then we would pause to get something to drink, or something to eat, but we kept on and kept on, and though I felt faint, there was a dogged strength in me, that last strength that people sometimes speak of. It is enormous—it is a boundless furious energy like shivering. I felt as I drove that I could not be halted, not by anything.

I wondered and wondered what would happen to my son when he grew old, if he grew old. I wondered if he would wear an unkempt beard, go about in pajamas. I wondered if he would feel some intensification of all he had known as the years passed, or whether things disparate would become more disparate still. I thought of rooms, quiet, dark rooms, with him sitting in them, facing sometimes towards the window, sometimes away, a window through which no light came. I thought of him walking on the scoured cement of shopping centers with plastic bags blowing past his knees, and his face dirty, his eyes tired. I thought of the place where he would die, perhaps a mattress, perhaps a stairwell. I thought of what he would feel at that moment, and to whom. In my mind it is my wife he calls to then, whether out loud or not, whether with some contortion of his trunk or not, whether crying with some wounded face, or staring blankly, a mind pushing on what is after all simply more nothing.

»

Outside of V, I woke in the night and my son was shouting. He was hitting the side of the car and shouting. I asked him what was wrong and he told me in his dream he was outside the upstairs bathroom in our house. He was standing on the carpet there, banging on the door. My wife was inside and he wanted to see her. She had been in there for too long, and she wouldn't come out. He had to see her.

I asked him when he had seen her last. When had that been?

He said he didn't know.

He started to say a time, but he stopped midway, and his hand fussed with the window crank. He pushed his face against the side of the door and closed his eyes.

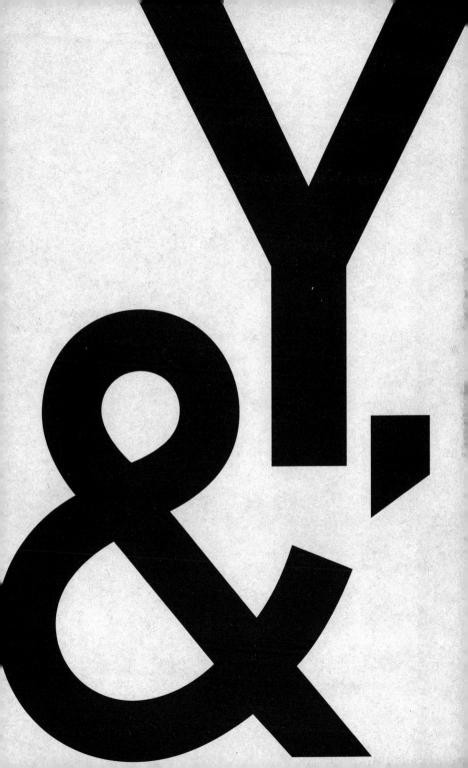

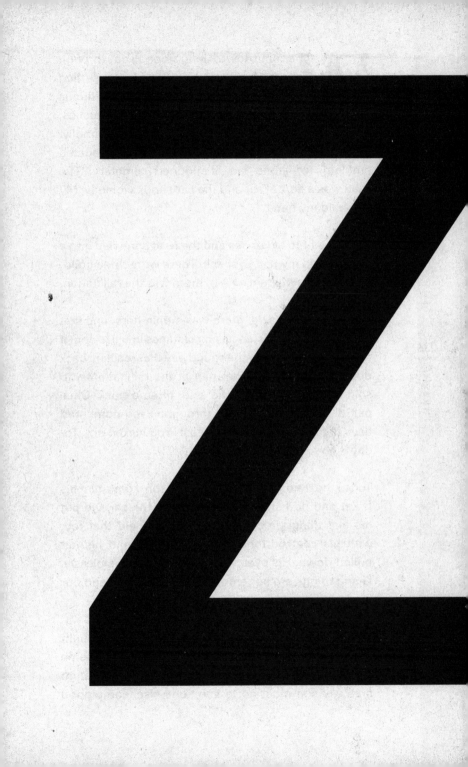

We came down a long slope all day through changing vegetation. Pine forest settled into the empty boughs of deciduous woods interpenetrated with bushes, some bright with leaves, with the red berries of holly. On the left away through the woods rose variegated emblems of stone—an abandoned cemetery. The road was a sort of rut and the car shook violently. My son held my hand.

We came onto a flatness and the road sprawled into a dismal little town, a flyspeck. There were three buildings and one of them, one of them was the railstation.

This was Z. As I said, there was a train here, one that shoots west any distance, any distance you like until it comes to the circuit—the roundway that reaches back down to the center. The man at the railstation who sold us my son's ticket, he said, three o'clock. Once per day the train comes through. Even-numbered days it goes west, odd-days east. You lucked out. Today it goes west.

Today the train goes west, I told my son. I gave him his ticket and he held it in his hand. At the car, we put his last things into his rucksack. He held that too, with his coat buttoned up to the chin and his hat pulled down. His eyes wandered my face helplessly. Living things are so remote. Our hearts leap and our bodies wait helplessly in space.

I thought to myself, I can be of no use to him. I thought once, I dreamed we would go together, as on some joined raft. My wife, my son, I. But this I, it must go first. My son must go to someone else, some good beginning, a place where a person can stay. Is there no such place?

I thought to myself, then, it is possible, the good *is* possible. It must be.

»

The train has left. It must be five or six, for the sky is darkening. The train has gone and with it my son.

I am weary and it is easy to sit down and so I do. Beside me is a ditch.

My son is gone. The train is gone, and with it my son.

My good death can't be more than a few minutes away. I feel a change in my eyes, something I can't describe, something unfamiliar. I know I should get down into the hole, and not make someone else do it for me. But, I don't want to go down there, not yet. I who have stood over so many bodies, so many dead bodies, so many old ailing bodies, soon to be dead, just dead, long dead, I in this body am confused in my consent.

My son stood on the metal step of the train and his whole self was open, was reaching to me. I who had buttoned all the buttons of his coat. I who had tucked his hair back. I moved my hand and it was some kind of waving that happened, a thing with no meaning. How could anything have meaning then? He looked at me and I know he knew what I had said—that I was going in a hole, that I would be no more. That he could never look for me. But what he knew about that—what it was to him to hear those things or say them again to himself: I do not even glimpse.

I smell the wet black dirt and remember days in the garden, when it would have been possible to stand and run to my wife or stand and run to my son. But I did not do so. I concerned myself with parsley or yams or pulling weeds. I had so much and all at once. There is too much light in those thoughts. Light everywhere. It obliterates me. I recoil.

My grave and my grave and my grave.

I am afraid, for I know there is no one there to speak to, no one to see. *There is no one in the hole.* All those things I thought might happen—they cannot happen there. No one is waiting for me down in that hole.

Once I came to get my son from school and when I arrived he was at the corner of the asphalt playground, and a few boys were there with him. They were leaning towards him in an awful way, and he was leaning into the fence. Perhaps his eyes even were closed—I was too far away to tell. One of the boys was saying things to him, and the other boys were shaking, I guess they were laughing. I came to the edge of the playground and called his name, I called to him, and the boys broke away. They walked off, past me, and they were so happy, with a kind of pure happiness of youth—a happiness that isn't good, that isn't evil, that exceeds all—and as I came towards my son he stayed there, leaning against the fence, his hand clutching a piece of old vine that was curled in the metal links. I called to him again, and again, and when I said his name right next to him he came.

There is so much that was terrible, and of it, I can never say how much of it he felt.

And now there is a future, his and not mine; I imagine it all, but somehow in my mind I do not picture his return, he will go somewhere else, somewhere farther. My son will travel all day on the train to the circuit station and at that station he will change to the next train and he will travel day and day and day—many days to the place where he goes. After many days, after an almost impossible distance, the train will stop at a little station near nothing. It will have to travel that far—until it is almost near nothing. The train will halt, grinding its metal brakes. The conductor will look around. The conductor will find my son in the seat he has chosen, a window seat from which he will be looking out. My son will be used by then to the traveling. He will have become fond of the train. The conductor will help him up, will get his bag. They will go together to the exit. During the trip, a trip that will last months, maybe even years, the conductor will have become fond of my son. They will have become parts of the train, parts of the continuing travel. But, the time will have come to go; they will embrace. My son will step onto the platform and stand there. He will stand there. The train will pull away.

Someone will be waiting in a car and will run to him. It will be perhaps my father, or my mother or my wife. They will know each other. No one knows anyone like this—so well will they be acquainted, so deeply. They will leap into each other's arms. They will climb together into the car in their joy and ride a short way over green banks, and as they ride they will approach a house, the house where I was born, or the house where she, my wife, was born. It will be her parents there, or mine, or perhaps even I will be there. The car will arrive at the house and such a gladness will reign,

I can't even speak of it. My son will dash to each person and be received, and he will tell them all of his journey. He, who will be the only one remaining, his the true census, he whose eyes have seen all, whose heart has felt all, he will speak of it to them, and in that place, that impossible place, all that he says will be understood as it never has been—and will pass into something far above the brutal retching of this earth that bites with its mouth and spits with its teeth, this earth that never gives without taking.